MANIAC

Cordell Cross

REVISED ISBN - 978-0-9869503-0-8

MANIAC
By Cordell Cross
Revised Copyright 2011
Vanbrugh Management Ltd.

Vanbrugh Publishing
A Division of Vanbrugh Management Ltd.
PO Box 73038
Evergreen RO
Surrey, B.C., Canada V3R 0J2

E-mail: vanbrugh@telus.net

Cover Design –Jana Siller
(contact) japla2003@yahoo.ca

Website – Mark Siller - f2marksiller@gmail.com

Preface

Black water laden clouds are not novel in the Pacific Northwest. During autumn and winter, locals take or leave the dark sky without complaint. Some people complain these clouds hide the moon. When this happens, lonely souls nervously walking along dimly lit side streets become the targets of deranged individuals that cherish the dark and use it to their advantage.

When it pours, alleys become even darker, and sensible people stay indoors rather than risk vicious encounters with psychopaths lying in wait. Yes, normal folk feel so secure in the safety of their homes, they tend to forget they could be being watched through uncovered windows. That's right, just a tiny crack in the Venetian blinds, or leaving drapes or curtains slightly open can turn on hordes of *onlookers*. These disturbed peeping toms crouching in the shadows don't wish to be caught so they demand quiet. Only then can they hear the swarm of commanding voices inside their heads, telling them what to do with those nearest to them. Just like this schizophrenic's thoughts whenever his urge demanded him to stalk his *prey*.

Damn, they're loud. If I had a gun, I'd shoot those fucking cats. Nah, I wouldn't be able to see them. Oh, you don't think so ... well fuck you. Then again, I like cats. No I don't! Cats are like whores hiding in the shadows of the night. If I could, I'd shoot the bastards. What's that? Yeah I know it would be too noisy. Okay, okay, I'd strangle or smother them. You always know best. I said you always know best, didn't I? Leave me alone.

Shit, the wind's picked up and it's starting to rain. Rain, rain, rain ... that's all it ever does in this fuckin' city. Why don't I move again? But what if I want to move? What could you do about it? Nothin'. You couldn't do nothin'. Okay, okay, I didn't say I was movin', did I? Get off my fuckin' back! Did I say I was movin'? Get you're fuckin' head examined, like they examined mine. They thought they diagnosed me? Hah! I gave 'em the bullshit and they bought it. They thought they had me all figured out? Bullshit - they know zilch.

I wonder if anyone has seen me. Just the wails from those cats must have got people rushing to their windows. No, no, no, everything's all right. I've just got to relax, that's all. Yeah, slow down by taking deep breaths. That's it, just relax. Okay, I'm relaxing ... Leave me alone. Nobody's interested in lookin' out on a night like this, anyway. Besides, how could they see little old me dressed in dark clothes in this pitch-black alley? What was that? What the hell did you ask? What if they see my breath? Is that what you asked? What a silly fuckin' question. What if they see my breath? Sometimes you really piss me off, do you know that? They won't - they won't see it! I just have to keep calm and quit being so fucking neurotic. I love the word, neurotic; it means fuck all. All those so-called medical terms mean nothin'. Piss in a bottle and take a blood test. I should have pissed in their faces, the pricks, struttin' around in their white coats.

Damn, even in this downpour I'm sweating like a whore in a group bed. I can smell myself and I smell like shit. I don't stink like this when I'm away from her; why do I reek when she's so close? Why is this happening to me? Maybe they're right. Maybe I do have a chemical imbalance. Hah, a chemical imbalance in my brain. Indeed, I have a chemical imbalance, all right, but it's in my balls not my fucking head.

Hey, I take after you. You know that don't you? Oh, go ahead and laugh, but I do - you know I do. Without me, though, you'd be fuckin' nothin'.

I know this bitch is the cause of it. She's the cause of everything wrong in my life. She's just like the others, struttin' around swaying her ass. Ooh, nice one too. Yeah, yeah, yeah, yeah, yeah — a nice ass. she struts around like those other whores. She thinks she's so fucking perfect, I'd like to cut ... Whoa, there I go again. I've gotta get hold of myself. Take a deep breath and let it out slowly. Yeah, that's it, and another, and another. That's more like it. That's it ... I can feel my heart slowing down.

I must be a complete fuckin' idiot. I know I can't let her get to me like those others, but it's tough. I know ... you warned me and I didn't listen. I won't, I won't, I won't, I won't, I won't, I won't let her get to me anymore. You won't have to remind me of those other whores again, either. I simply have to get those sluts out of my mind! But I'll have her first; I'll have this bitch if I'm patient. All I have to do is bide my time. Yeah, that's it ... bide my time.

What the...? Where did he come from? I'll walk around him. Fuck off dog, before I give you a ... He's fast. That's it, fuck off and get yourself one of those cats.

What's that you say? Maybe Miss. Prim and Proper won't take her bath tonight? What if she took it yesterday? I'm reeking and soaked to the skin so she'd better fucking take it tonight. She'd better, she'd better, she'd better, she'd better fucking take it! If she doesn't, I'll smash the window and wring her fuckin' neck for what she's putting me through. No, I'll dissect her from vulva to mammillae, or maybe I'll just slit the bitch's throat and then dismember her.

Hey, what's the matter with me? I'm sorry. I said I'm sorry. Why don't I just settle down again and relax. Why am I getting so excited over another slut? I took care of the others didn't I? Just the way you told me to. Those fucking nymphets thinking they knew it all got everything they deserved. They knew fuck all when I got through with them. No siree, they won't bother me again, or anyone else for that matter. You're proud of me aren't you? I said, you're proud of me aren't you? Thank you ... Yeah, thanks for nothin' you fuckin' asshole.

The figure paused at a house, glanced around for a moment, and spoke quietly. "Shit, the light's not on in the bathroom. What's that? What will I do if it's not on in her bedroom? It will be on. I said it will be on. If it isn't I'll…"

After murmuring only a few more words, the figure's gloved right hand reached over the house's backyard gate. Heavy rain pelting against a giant old maple tree's leaves muffled the squeak of the gate's latch. Other than the drenching rain and two cats fighting in the distance, the only other sound was a rasping noise made by the wind gently pushing a tire rope swing rubbing one of the old maple's strong wet branches.

Leaving the gate wide open, the crouching intruder slowly scanned the area. He was alone except for the person who always watched him. That's if he was being watched. He didn't care. Perhaps his mind was playing tricks again. It didn't matter who wanted to watch as long as she was there waiting for him. She always waited for him behind her window. She knew he was there; of course she did. She had to know he was watching her; why else would she take off her clothes? She always teased him, wanting him to savour every square inch of the tight tanned skin that formed her breasts, and buttocks and legs.

Silently making his way along the moss-covered pathway the figure suddenly stopped again, thinking he had heard something other than the rain. Scanning from side to side and glancing behind him, he continued moving slowly towards the old weatherworn three-story red house with seven wooden steps leading to the back porch. He could see her light now. Only one basement light shone against the dark-green five-foot high fence running along the east side of the dwelling.

The trespasser's eyes opened wide and his face became determined seeing the light that originated from her bedroom. He'd seen it many times before. As he got closer those same eyes narrowed, his lips quivered, and his sweat mingled with the rain on his intense face. Moving slowly, an overwhelming stimulating sensation infused the region between his legs. This feeling was also a challenge; it felt so good he'd kill for it. Gritting his teeth, he felt aroused energy controlling every inch of his body. This tormenting excitement dominated all his senses and he knew it wouldn't stop. It never did when he was near her. In a few minutes, she would allow him to be within a few feet. She wanted him as much as he wanted her, but right now, she just wanted him to watch.

When the kitchen light came on, the *invader* instantly stopped breathing. Turning his face away from the house, he quickly moved to crouch by the fence. The kitchen light now illuminated the worn unpainted stairs and the wooden fire escape ladder atop those stairs. Shortly, he would use this ladder to lead him to a small landing outside the bathroom window on the second floor.

The man's craving heightened even more when the kitchen light went out and he cautiously stood and lowered a hood over his face. This was his moment, and the feeling between his legs made him want cry out and rip her apart. Oh, God, he had been waiting for this. The sensation was ecstasy on earth, and she created it only for him. Yes, only he could feel such euphoria.

Moving quietly under the eaves towards the basement window forced his heart to race, allowing his thick gushing blood to strain every vein and artery. He was nearly there and now and he could see the one-inch opening between the curtains. His heart pounded, and his tongue couldn't provide enough liquid to moisten his lips and mouth. He wanted to cough but he daren't and now his once sweaty wet face had dried and felt sticky under the wool cover.

Wearing her dressing gown, fifteen-year-old Sandra Potts hummed softly moving her giant brown teddy bear from its reigning position amidst her bed pillows to a chair by the window which was open an inch.

The perfectly proportioned five-foot-four teenager with her pinned up golden hair could hear the rain outside her uniquely decorated room. She liked the sound of rain, particularly when she was in her warm bed. It made her feel like she was in a cabin in the wild. In the summer, her cabin's open window caught the warm breezes and sweet smelling flower fragrances. Not now, though. With winder coming on, she only left her window open an inch. If she opened it wider, her room would be cold from the wind gusting against the fence.

Sandra loved her room. She had decorated it herself with wallpaper depicting watercolours of birds in flight. It was her special little abode; cool in the summer, warm in the winter, and it had its own entrance.

The girl had just finished her homework and upon turning down the bedclothes, her telephone rang. A knowing smile stretched her lips as she sat on her bed and picked up the device. "Hello you."

When a male voice said, "Hi, Sandy," the beautiful girl's smile widened. Sandra's boyfriend Philip Bayer usually telephoned her every night around this time, and if he didn't, he heard about it the next day at school.

"Hi, Phil. Well, did you buy it?"

"You bet, but it cost me twenty-two bucks."

"Philip Bayer, how can you justify working your butt off in that restaurant for three hours just to blow your money on The Rejecters?"

"Sandy, haven't you heard? *Get Outta my Face* is the number one song on the charts. You can bet it's really cool! Totally cool."

Sandra giggled, saying, "It has to be if El Cheapo spends twenty two dollars on it. Yeah, I like it too. It's totally nice."

The boy raised his voice a bit. "Hey, who's El Cheapo? I took us out for steaks, didn't I?"

"True, but the whole evening didn't cost half of what you spent on The Rejecters."

Philip deepened his voice and tried to talk high-class. "Are you sayin' I should get my priorities straight, Miss. Sandra Potts?"

The girl really liked Philip although they hadn't known each other that long. Subconsciously winding the telephone's cord around her right hand, she chirped, "Something like that."

"What are you doing, Sandy?"

"I've finally finished my homework and I'm going up to take a bath."

The boy chuckled. "Can I come over and wash your ... back?"

Wearing a bashful grin, Sandra replied, "No you can't, Philip Bayer, and I've got to go. Are you picking me up for school tomorrow?"

"Duh, hello, hello, Sandy? There is no school tomorrow - it's Saturday. You've been spending too much time reading those birdbrain books of yours. Don't you remember we were gonna go to a movie tonight, but I got called in to work?"

A confused look came over Sandra and she gently slapped her forehead. "What's happening to me? I must be totally out of it. I wonder if it's all this rain. Also, my books are about birds. They're not birdbrain books, Buster. Will you be at the barbecue tomorrow?"

"You bet," Philip replied. "Well, gotta go, the boss is callin' me. Goodnight Babe."

The dark figure's wild eyes widened watching the girl make a kissing motion into the telephone before placing it down.

A few moments later, Sandra stood glancing around the room before picking up a small portable radio and taking a white nightdress out of a drawer. With the garment tucked under her left arm and the radio held tightly in her left hand, the girl looked around the room again before turning out the light.

Not wanting to take any chances, the figure quickly pulled his head back when the light went out. He knew if his *prey* had remained in the dark room, she might have seen his silhouette.

More than aware of the girl's destination, the man's lips formed an insidious smirk as he slowly edged towards the end of the house. For two agonizing days, he'd fantasized about this moment. Once again, another crucial tick in time would allow his mind to shape every possible erotic desire.

The sky opened a little more and the kitchen light went on and off as the intruder silently climbed the backstairs. They creaked a little, but not the fire escape ladder he used to climb to the landing outside of the unlit bathroom window.

A crack in the roof's gutter kept an irregular flow of water drumming against the intruder's neck and back but he didn't feel the cold liquid; his exploding body and brain wouldn't permit interruptions to his vicious concentration.

Suddenly a light came on and the crouching trespasser saw Sandra Potts place her radio and nightdress on a chair before turning on the bathtub's giant taps and standing in the doorway speaking with someone. Over the sound of gushing steamy water, he could barely hear her voice saying, "That's totally okay because I'm eating in the school's cafeteria on Monday anyway. Goodnight."

While the tub filled, the teenager shook out her shoulder-length hair, locked the door, tuned in her favourite radio station and hummed with the music while curtseying in front of a large wall mirror.

Sandra also liked this room, especially on nights like this. The steam made it warm and cosy and she could react with the mirror and be anyone she wanted. The girl wasn't concerned that one bent slat on the Venetian blind opened the whole room to prying eyes - eyes nearly pressed against the rising condensation engulfing a small region outside the window. After all, who would have the nerve to enter the yard, walk up the back stairs and climb the fire escape in this deluge, or at any other time? She felt comforted knowing her dad was down below watching television. He could hear like an elephant and if anyone did try to climb the stairs, it would be their last climb. Yes, this was her second favourite room, and for the next half-hour, she could relax and be a rock star, a movie star, or act like the teenage models she admired.

After forming umpteen hairstyles, Sandra pulled down the shoulders of her gown and pushed up her breasts. She had seen the video Gone with the Wind, and every angled come-on pose made her feel more and more like Scarlet O'Hara. Slowly unzipping the garment to her waist, the girl allowed it to gently slide over her upper body, defiantly baring her heaving pink breasts to an imaginary Rhett Butler about to pick her up in his arms. Raising her chin higher, *Scarlet* and *Rhett* watched the remainder of the dressing gown delicately glide over her smooth curvaceous hips and fall to the floor.

The intruder's intense gaze took in every inviting morsel of Sandra's lightly bronzed and beautifully proportioned body. With each quickening breath, his twitching hands wanted to break the window, caress her, kiss her, crush her, and then feel the struggling girl's last heartbeat as she fought in vain to wrench his muscular hands from her throat. Turning off the taps and turning up the radio, the naked girl returned to the mirror and using a small scrub-brush for a microphone gyrated while miming the Rejecters new hit *Get Outta my Face*. When the song ended, the *singer* elegantly strolled to the bathtub, poured in some bubble bath, stroked the water with both hands and climbed in.

While dancing, Sandra had not heard the sensual moaning sounds of the demented man outside her window. Nor had she heard him nimbly climb down and disappear into the night. A half-hour later though, while drinking a glass of milk she peered through the window in the kitchen door. "Hey Dad, when you put the garbage out, you totally forgot to close the gate."

Chapter 1

"What kind of rum is this?" Greg Britton asked, wincing while peering through a glass he held up to a light. "Don't tell me the club's using those cheap brands again?"

"It's Lemon Heart, sir. You like the imported rums; well you're drinking Lemon Heart," the golf club's young bartender shot back after displaying the bottle he had poured from seconds earlier. Bringing the bottle to the bar, he added, "Mr. Britton, you haven't been drinking very much lately; you've forgotten what real rum tastes like."

Britton and his regular golf-playing friends, Jim Potts, Larry Sumislouski and Wayne Laidlaw had just finished playing a round of golf and had decided to have a few drinks before heading home.

There weren't too many people sitting in the old colonial style clubhouse. Normally the well-furnished room with photographs of every world famous golfer adorning the walls would have been packed but for the wet weather. The previous night's downpour had turned into a morning

Scottish mist keeping only a handful of brightly coloured caps and golf umbrellas unfurled throughout the soggy links. Although many complaints had circulated over the years about the bright orange colour of the club's golf hats and umbrellas, members didn't hesitate wearing the caps and opening up the umbrellas on days like this.

On wet days, most members stayed home rather than getting soaked playing their favourite game, but not the club's devoted golfers. At one time, some of the real enthusiasts had even asked the manager to allow them to use black balls when light snow fell. When they were turned down, they couldn't believe it and threatened to have him fired. Common sense eventually ruled that out.

Leaving his drink on the bar, Britton rolled his eyes to the ceiling before he gave the bartender a suspicious look and delivered two drinks and a beer to his seated friends who were now in deep conversation. Strolling back to the bar, he picked up his drink, placed both elbows on the counter and leaned forward. "Son, how old do you think I am? Not how old do you think I look, but how old do you think I am? Be honest now. Would you say I'm in my twenties, thirties, forties, or fifties?"

A tiny grin appeared before the young bartender said, "Do you want a truthful answer, Mr. Britton?"

The grin became contagious. "Yeah, that's what I said. You look like an intelligent person ... how old do I look."

"Well, sir ... you're a bit overweight."

Greg cleared his throat. "True. I know I have a bit of a gut, but I can still do a mile in nine-and-a-half minutes. I could probably outrun you."

"I doubt that, sir. And you're losin' some hair."

"It happens when you're a cop and you're past thirty. Whoops, I've given you a hint of the answer, haven't I? Anyway, wait till you reach my age."

"And you've got a bit of a double chin," the barkeep added, still grinning.

"What are you now - a would-be plastic surgeon? Out with it."

Slowly stroking his cleanly-shaven cheeks and chin, the bartender cocked his head and agreeably volunteered, "Thirty-five, er, give or take a year?"

Greg laughed and remained smiling broadly as he quickly stood up straight and wrapped both his hands around the grinning bartender's right hand. "Right on, and because you're such an honest fella you won't have to remind me to tip you. Has anyone every told you to enter politics?"

"No, sir, they haven't."

"Well you should. It's quite obvious this old world needs people like you."

"Thank you, Mr. Britton. But what's your age got to do with the rum, sir?"

"Well your *gestimate* of my age is out by about twenty years, so I should know what the hell I'm drinking. You see, young man, I'm a rum connoisseur. I was raised on that beautiful black liquid of the Gods. You could blindfold me and if I smelled the bottle, I'd be able to tell you what brand it is."

"Wow, how's your liver, sir?"

"So now you're a doctor? Listen, someone has tampered with that bottle. It's not Lemon Heart, and if it is, it's been watered down. You'd better pour me a Lamb's Navy Rum. I'll let you know if *that* bottle has also been meddled with."

A few moments later while the bartender sniffed the questionable Lemon Heart container, Britton picked up his new drink, sipped it, indicated it was fine, and sauntered back to his table. Halfway, he glanced over his shoulder and said, "That's it - check it out and you'll see I'm right."

"What was that all about?" Britton's friend Dr. Larry Sumislouski asked as Greg sat down. "Are you pulling the old free drink ruse on the young bartenders again, Britton?"

All four golfers chuckled glancing at each other. Each remembered a time back when they had 'sucked in' this barman when he had first arrived. The bad booze ruse had gotten them quite a few free drinks.

"Nah, he's probably still paying off our bill," Greg said, stretching and holding his glass up to the light again. "I was just suggesting that someone's watering down the liquor again. Things don't change, do they? I know I haven't had a drink in awhile, but any three year old could have handled that last drink he served me. Someone should mention this to the manager."

"Maybe it's the manager that's stealing or drinking the stuff," Jim Potts said, tongue in cheek. "Say, I wonder if he's watering down the non alcoholic beer?"

When Wayne Laidlaw said, "I'm quite happy just seeing you out having a drink," Greg didn't respond and after all their eyes met, the other three left it at that.

Larry Sumislouski cleared his throat and changed the subject. "Er, Mrs. Grant spoke with me when I was bringing in my garbage cans this morning."

Greg winced again sipping his new drink. The booze tasted fine but he'd heard the words, "Mrs. Grant," the widow who lived across the alley from Larry Sumislouski and Jim Potts.

"Good old Mrs. Grant, Greg said. I'd speak to her but there's no speaking to old Madge. What's she bitching about now? Is my cat still sneaking in her house and pissing everywhere on her early American antique furniture, or grabbing her Sunday roast and bringing it to me? I should ask her to join the police force - her eyes and nose never miss a thing."

"Sunday roast?" Potts asked, grinning.

Greg's smile widened. "Yeah. Each Sunday she cooks a small roast. She wraps it in string, and then takes it out of the oven to cool. Well, my cat, Mickey, entered her house, stole her roast, and dragged it home. She chased him with a broom but he was too fast for her. Hey, I get a lot of food brought home. Mickey's a thief."

Laidlaw roared out laughing. "Did you give it back?"

"Hell no. She's a great cook. Certainly I gave it back; I'm not going to keep the old gal's roast."

"What did she do with it?" Larry asked, grinning like the rest.

"She said she'd wash it off and heat it up. I gave her five bucks just to stop her from cursing Mickey. Was she bitching about me again?"

Larry grinned shaking his head. "No, she, er, appeared friendly for a change. Go easy on her, Greg ... Madge is seventy-nine and actually a good neighbour. If it weren't for her, I'd never have caught that son-of-a-bitch stealing my flowers. Oh, by the way ... Jim, what time did you go to bed last night?"

Sandra's dad finished his beer and lightly burped. "About eleven o'clock ... why?"

"Madge thought she saw someone in your yard."

Jim Potts' eyes became slits. "What? What time?"

"She wasn't exactly sure. Around ten-fifteen, ten-thirty."

"It was me putting the garbage out," Jim replied, his face taking on its normal robust look again. "Who wants another drink?"

"Christ, that old broad never misses a thing," Laidlaw stated. "Is she our Block Watch rep?"

"Ours? I think she watches every block in the city," Greg offered, finishing his drink and handing his glass to Jim. "Make mine Lamb's, not Lemon Heart."

Not quite finished, Sumislouski asked, "Did you also leave your gate open?"

"Yeah, I must have," Jim Potts said, standing. "Yeah, yeah I did ... Sandy pointed it out last night. Well, don't all thank me at once; who wants another drink besides Greg?"

"That Gosling boy could have been in your yard last night and you'd never have known it," Wayne said, his face displaying critical countenance just thinking about the two men living one house away from Madge and across the alley from Greg.

"Why do you call him a boy? Sumislouski asked. "I hear he's in his middle to late thirties and at one time he was a damned good surgeon. Even though he was a specialist, he also maintained a general practice."

Greg passed Wayne's glass to Potts. "We've known Ronnie Gosling since he started university, that's why. Now he's nothing more than a vegetable, and whatever illness he has, it's progressing. Before you moved here, Larry, it was a big deal for this club to have one of its distinguished members … the eminent Doctor Ronald Gosling, return to play a round. The place would be packed because the world-famous heart surgeon was holidaying in his hometown and playing golf."

Wayne's face remained firm. "Yeah, but that was then. Now he gives me the willies. Whenever I'm in my garden or the alley, I always see their curtains moving and I know I'm being watched. I can feel that son-of-a-bitch's eyes observing every move I make."

"Ever since his son went off his rocker, old man Gosling watches him closely," Potts said, standing up to buy the drinks. "Actually, I haven't seen Vern or Ronnie in over a month. Their front grass needs cutting."

Larry Sumislouski glanced up after checking his scorecard. "Their front grass? Have you seen their vegetable garden out back? It looks like the city dump."

"I know what you're thinking, Wayne, but Ronnie Gosling was never charged," Greg said, sitting back. "We know he's more mentally slow now and he's probably got a multitude of other problems, but he was never charged with raping and killing those girls in Olympia where he had his office."

"He had offices everywhere," Sumislouski said, finishing his drink. "And from what I've read he was a brilliant surgeon … perhaps too brilliant. Some of his surgical methods are still praised to this day. He might not have been charged, Greg, but I'd lay odds he did them in."

"Well, we can all relax," Britton said, pounding his right fist on the table. "The two live next door but one to Madge and she'd never let them get away with anything. Wayne, if you think Ronnie and Vern Gosling are watching you, check out Madge's moving curtains the next time you're in your backyard. I do, and although I can't see her, I wave at her house, asking 'Is my cat over there pissing on your furniture, Madge, my dear?' It never fails. Every time I wave, I see her curtains move. She also gives me dirty looks when she hangs out her laundry, or passes me in the alley, or while shopping at our local stores."

"That's reverse acknowledgement," Larry said with a grin that burst into a robust laugh. "She's got the hots for you, that's all. She might be in her late seventies, Greg, but she'd be able to teach you a few things."

The four neighbours laughed aloud and over the next half-hour discussed their scores, golf game, lives, cars, world affairs and the neighbourhood. All of them knew old Madge guarded her reputation as the block busybody, and as they got up to leave, Jim Potts stated, "Well, someone's gotta keep their eyes open, we've all got kids."

"Speak for yourself," Britton responded. "The only pitter-patter of little feet I wanna hear are my mice, and I've told Mickey to sort them out when he's not having a pissing parade, or he's with his cat barbershop quartet over at Madge's house."

Larry Sumislouski's grin widened again. "When those four goddamned cats are fighting, no one in our house can get to sleep. It's even worse during the wee hours of the morning. Please keep your cat in at night, Greg, and maybe the other owners will do the same. A few nights back they were on Madge's porch and she came out with a bucket of water and let them have it. Boy that woman can curse."

"Yeah, and I don't think you should mimic her," Jim Potts said, reminding his friends that the Salvation Army frowns on bad language.

"Sorry, Jim, Larry said, displaying a touch of repentance.

Time flew as the four chums chuckled again about things happening in their neighbourhood. When they were ready to walk out the door the barman called them back for a photograph. Moments later they had their arms around each other with the bartender muttering, "Say, cheese."

"Sayin' sex is better," Greg quipped, trying not to move his lips.

"Times must be tough when this club starts taking pictures for birdies," Jim said, before pointing his hand at Larry. "He got it, so just take his mug shot."

Sumislouski raised both forefingers to the corners of his mouth and feigned a forced extended smile. "I like my friends in my pictures. Snap it up, will ya?"

The bartender did, but the flash didn't work.

"You've got friends? Jim asked.

Wayne expressed a questioning look. "If it was a birdie."

"I'll ignore those statements," Sumislouski said, offering to help the barman, and advising, "It works better if you use batteries."

Embarrassed, the young bartender rushed away to get fresh batteries while the four sat down again and Greg drained the last drop out from his glass. "When I sank that birdie two weeks ago, no one took my picture."

Larry cast a doubtingly glance at Greg. "It was an eagle, that's why. This is an honest club, Britton."

"Oh really? Well I think we'd better tell that to whoever's waterin' down the booze."

After the barkeep took two pictures and the trio left the building, Wayne sighed, saying "On the wall with a million others. When is a hero going to emerge amongst us and shoot a hole-in-one?"

Greg's response, "Gimmee a couple of weeks," earned him a sore back from all their patting.

On the way home in the detective's station wagon, Larry Sumislouski got what he knew was coming when Wayne said to him, "Marrying late and starting a family doesn't qualify you to screw around with us old reprobates, you know?"

The driver agreed with Laidlaw but didn't agree with the word old. "Hey, who's old? You two speak for yourselves."

Although considerably younger than the others, Sumislouski managed to stand up for himself. "Eat your hearts out … a birdie's a birdie. I'll collect at the barbecue, thank you."

"You're not collecting from me until I check out that ball," Potts stated trying to keep a straight face.

Acting aghast, Sumislouski said, "What? Jim, you sit there and accuse me, your dentist, and your best next door neighbour of…?"

"My last filling fell out."

"Bullshit! It came out because you chomped on a bone." Sumislouski offered, raising his voice slightly.

Laidlaw got into the act, saying, "Larry, you began with an Airflight, and finished up with a Palmer. I'm with Jim … I ain't payin' until I also see that ball. How about you, Greg?'

Britain chuckled, saying, "I'm with you two."

Smiles filled all faces when Larry said, "What the hell are you talking about? I started with a Palmer ball. What's with this Airflight BS? My wife told me Diane was the only person that ever … used … Airfl…"

Sumislouski stopped in the middle of his sentence. He knew he'd blundered and didn't need Jim to poke him or Wayne to grimace as he did. Diane had been Greg's wife until getting sick. After the funeral, it had taken the three of them four months to get Greg just slightly close to normal or even out of his house.

Swallowing, and deeply regretful, Larry said, "Sorry, Greg, I … I didn't mean to bring back memories."

The others might not have seen Greg's lost look or rapid eyelid movements. The detective had turned his head to make certain they didn't. "That's okay, Larry," he said. "Six months is a long time, and I'm getting over it. Besides, Diane used Farshoots."

Just to ease the situation a little, Jim asked, "Uh, Wayne, what time's the barbecue?"

"Six-thirty's fine."

The four never said much during the last ten minutes of the ride while the Heavens opened and the windshield wipers acted as mesmerising metronomes.

Greg felt a little uncomfortable knowing his friends found themselves walking on eggshells. There was no need for Larry to apologize after mentioning Diane's name. Time had changed all that, at least in public. Only in the quietness of his house when his wandering mind disobeyed his subconscious orders and locked on Diane's name or an object she loved, did he break down and search life's encyclopaedia of "why." Why would God take a person that never said a bad word about anyone? Why would He want to take away the kind of person that would use a piece of paper to take a lost or nomadic ant off the steps and place it gently on a leaf or back on the ground?

Snap out of it, Greg, he finally said to himself. They're great friends and neighbours. They shouldn't have to walk the gauntlet between my memories. Besides, I wouldn't know what to do without them. The four of us help each other out so often our alliance is like an extended family. I'm glad we introduced ourselves all those years ago. Living so close and having so many mutual interests is wonderful.

Just as the rain stopped and he established his friends shouldn't be suffering with him, Greg turned into the alley running north/south behind their houses and pulled up at the rear of Jim and Helen Potts' home, the first house on the south/west side of the lane, across from Madge's house. Larry and Joan Sumislouski's residence lay in between the Potts' dwelling and Greg's house, and Wayne and Glenda Laidlaw lived on the other side of the police lieutenant's house. The Laidlaws had recently built a swimming pool and it was a first for the old neighbourhood. That afternoon, rain or shine, Wayne and Glenda were throwing a pool initiation barbecue in their back yard. They had even erected a tent just in case it rained.

Like most houses in the area, all four residences had been built in the early 1930s and had been well maintained. Only Larry Sumislouski and Greg Britton's lots had wooden garages with doors opening onto the alley. Jim and Wayne parked their cars on the north side of their lots at the front.

"These clouds are parting so we may just get lucky," Britton said, getting out and opening the rear door so his friends could retrieve their golf bags.

The others indicated they agreed and took interest when Greg got back in his car and commented on the worn looking 1949 Ford sitting with its hood up in Sumislouski's open garage. "Larry, are you still working on that thing?"

"Thing? Why are you calling it *a thing*?" Sumislouski asked, picking up a nearby rag and proudly wiping the car's front bumper. "In two months you'll be begging me for a ride."

"You're probably right. Reminds me of an old squad car I used to drive. Yeah, those were the days, all right. Talk about power. Well, see you guys at six-thirty."

While Greg slowly drove forward and parked his vehicle in his garage, Wayne walked behind in the alley and turned his head, saying, "Hey, Larry, if I taste axle grease on my next visit, I'm gonna change dentists."

"Smart ass," Larry replied, chuckling with Jim Potts as the two men entered their own back yards.

"Wanna come in for a drink, Greg?" Wayne asked, as Britton was about to close his garage doors. "We've got your favourite, Lemon Heart, and I'll guarantee it's not watered down."

Greg gratefully declined, saying, "Thanks anyway, Wayne, but I'm expecting a call from Jeff."

"Ah, our number one law student. How's he doing?"

The detective didn't want it to appear, but the lost look returned. "Not bad, but ... he misses his mother, and..."

"You miss him as well?"

Greg's eyes stared at the ground. "Yeah."

Displaying a sympathetic smile, Wayne set his golf bag down. "Listen, Greg, you've had too much time on your hands since Diane passed away. Six months off work hasn't been good for you. Have you thought about going back?"

"I keep busy."

"I know that, but are you going back?"

Greg's eyes turned more distant and he fought to stop them from welling up. "I don't think so," he said, before his voice cracked and changed to a whisper. "Wayne, this thing has killed me. I still don't know what I'm doing half the time."

Wayne Laidlaw exhibited sorrow for his friend. He knew Diane had been Greg's life and vice-versa. Sickness had ripped apart the resilient spirit of an eternally devoted couple, leaving one partner to wander alone and at times asking, begging, even demanding to join his lost love.

"Greg ... at my age I think I know what you're going through and I don't have any answers. No one has ... except maybe God, and he's playing a hand he doesn't want you to see right now for whatever reason. He's eventually going to show it, but at this moment, he's indicated he wants you living, and I'm certain he wants your pain to cease. However, that can only happen when you occupy your mind with other interests. Good cops are hard to find, old friend. Surely you miss the excitement of the department?"

"Not really. I'm doing just fine visiting the cemetery rather than punching a time-clock."

Wayne sensitively acknowledged Greg's statement. "Did you go there today?"

"Earlier."

"Have you ever missed a day?"

"No, why?"

Picking up his golf bag, Laidlaw replied, "No reason. Are you sure you don't want to come in for a drink?"

When Greg smiled and shook his head, Wayne said, "Don't forget, six-thirty?"

"I'll be there. Want me to bring some beer or wine?"

Wayne motioned Greg to close the garage doors and they would talk to each other over their fence. A few moments later he said, "Greg, do I bring liquor to your get-togethers?"

"I dunno, do ya? It's been a while since we ... since I threw a party."

"Just bring yourself," Wayne said, displaying serene eyes and a compassionate smile. "Glenda's done all the shopping."

After casually waving, both men headed towards their houses, and as Greg climbed the back stairs to his enclosed porch, Wayne entered his home through the basement door.

Britton had no sooner placed his golf bag down, taken out his keys and opened the door when his black and white cat Mickey ran up the stairs and began rubbing his body against his owner's left leg.

"Hello, Mickey. Yeah, I know it's lunchtime. Let's go get you somethin'."

For some reason, houses tend to assume the mood of their occupants, and Greg Britton's residence was no exception. Spotlessly clean and furnished with finesse, the place now seemed sterile and apathetic to habitation. When Diane lived, it was always friendly and devoted to all who entered. On weekends, the smell of freshly baked bread, pies, and scones filled the air along with the succulent aroma of Sunday's roast. While Diane pottered around improving the character of the charming old wooden building, Greg attended to the million-and-one odd jobs the aged house demanded.

Greg Britton had lived in his house a long time, and the dwelling was getting on even when he and Diane had moved in. To Greg it seemed just like yesterday, yet it was so long ago. Now things were different and he noticed the change of ambience the second he entered the lonely kitchen. He always strained his ears anyway, waiting to hear four familiar words he knew would never be asked again. "Is that you, dear?"

After closing the door, the police officer dropped his keys on the kitchen table and upon noticing a blinking red light on his telephone answering machine, pressed the button.

"Hi, Dad, it's me. I'll call you later," his son's voice announced.

Mickey continued rubbing Greg's legs before the detective opened a lower cupboard and took out a box of dry cat food. After spreading some in Mickey's dish and returning the box, Greg strolled through the hallway and living room then opened the front door and picked up his morning newspaper. It was midpoint of the first month of autumn and the road's magnificent giant elms lining both sides of the street provided an apple green cathedral ceiling. Presently the trees were only allowing bits of the sky to peek through, but Greg saw nature's coming disrobing act. Soon, the leaves would turn crimson, yellow, and brown, and in a month or so, he knew only a skeleton framework of huge branches would tower over the street. Spring and summer's ceiling would lie in the gutters or get raked from front yards and set afire by residents who had mowed their lawns for the last time a few weeks before.

Just down the block, some boys had set up two nets and an exciting game of street hockey attracted local fans. A sentimental smile came to Greg's face as he watched the game for a few minutes. When Diane was alive, he remembered her saying, "One day they're playing street hockey. Next, they're getting married, and soon after that, their kids are playing street hockey."

The thought made Greg take a good look at his front lawn and garden still bearing the signs of Diane's loving care. Since his wife's death Greg had only used the front gate once, and that was three days ago when he had raked the leaves. Before that, he couldn't even look at the front of his house. He knew he would break down from the many memories of seeing Diane on her knees amongst her flowers, humming to them with the music flowing from a portable radio she always placed on the front porch. Recently, Wayne Laidlaw and Larry Sumislouski had been kind enough to mow the lawn and tidy up his front garden. The lawn at the back of the house was a different story. Greg kept it looking like a putting green complete with a fluttering flag at the lone hole he and his neighbours used for putting practices and bets.

When the telephone rang, Greg closed the front door and headed back to the kitchen. As he picked up the phone and sat down, his newspaper unfurled.

"Hello."

"Hi, Dad – how's it going?"

"Better, now that you've phoned, Son," Greg replied, his face brightening. "Did you pass your exams?"

"Aced 'em, Pop. At least I think I did."

"So you like this summer rotation thing?"

"Yeah, it's different. All universities should try it. It'll give me more time to spend at home."

The police officer's fingers toyed with his keys as his eyes scanned the headline jumping off the newspaper's front page. *Rapist Still At Large!*

"Great. So, we've finally got a lawyer in the family, eh?"

"Three more years will tell, Dad. Uh, is ... is it getting any easier for you?"

Greg knew the boy was putting on a front. His mother's death had torn him apart as well. "I think so, Jeff. How are you holding out?"

"Okay, I guess. Dad, have you opened the drapes, blinds and windows?"

"What?"

"Mom always had them open, but when I came home for the funeral, you kept them closed."

"I'm getting around to it, Son," Greg said, knowing they remained closed and feeling guilty about lying. When Diane lived and the sun shone, most windows were open and the sounds of the neighbourhood entered with the breeze and its fragrances. The house was a sounding board of lawn mowers, outside radios, and laughing children blending with the regular ice-cream truck's musical notes and the clippety-clop of Noddy, the junkman's old horse. Rain or shine, Noddy always looked forward to receiving a carrot and a pat from Diane. She loved that old horse immensely, and he loved her.

If somehow she missed feeding Noddy, she'd walk a mile to give him his carrot. Although he was hard of hearing and wore blinders, her "friend" always knew when Diane was near.

Greg bowed his head as tears filled his eyes. He knew he tried to keep up the carrot tradition whenever he could, and Noddy appreciated it but never seemed to tire of looking around for Diane.

"That's a good sign, Dad. Uh, you're in the middle of a million memories there, so … why not sell the place?"

Clearing his throat and swallowing, Greg wiped his eyes. "Your mother wouldn't want that, Jeff. You were born here and … well …I …" Tears blurred the newspaper headline, and after taking a heavy breath he murmured, "Are you still there, Jeff?"

"I'm here, Dad."

"…I feel your mother is still here with us."

Britton could hear a nasal resonance in Jeff's soft voice, and he heard his son sniffing. "Dad, for some reason I played Mom's favourite song today."

"I do the same, Jeff. Er, when will you be home?"

"I'm still writing finals; probably a month. I like these August classes. Uh, I … er … wish I could ease your grief, Dad."

Greg could barely hear his son's last words so he knew the boy was still taking his mother's death hard. "Listen, Charlie Brown, we're a couple of fighters, you and me. Call me when you're on your way."

"I will, Dad … take care."

After saying, "God bless, Jeff - I love you," and placing the telephone down, the police officer just stared at the device for a good thirty seconds. During that brief moment, a myriad of the toughest, dirtiest cases he'd ever been assigned ran through his mind. He had seen every cruel and inhuman act possible and experienced the unbelievable pain and violent suffering that comes with the assignments his job demanded. But all of that combined could not compare to the agony he was now going through, and he wondered if it would ever stop. Every time he sat at the kitchen table, his mind asked the same questions: What if he hadn't become a cop? What if he had just coached junior football, or become a physical education instructor? If he hadn't joined the force, he would have spent more time with Diane, that's for sure. Moreover, what about all those nights he walked the beat knowing she was alone, worrying. Funny, she always worried when I was on the night shift. Most crime takes place during the day, yet Diane didn't like me working nights.

Greg wiped his eyes with his handkerchief, picked up Mickey and his newspaper and walked into the living room, murmuring "Oh, Di, maybe I really should have stayed coaching college football. If I had, I could have spent more time with you. A lot more time with you, Sweetheart."

"No, you knew I wanted to be a cop and you supported me at every turn," he said, finally snapping out of his spell.

After placing the cat on the couch and the newspaper on the arm of his favourite chair, the police officer turned on the polished old stereo, took a record out of its sleeve and placed it on the turntable. Even this action made him think of Diane. Neighbours and friends had advised them to buy a CD player, but Diane had her record collection and that was that.

As Della Reese's voice singing *Don't You Know* filled the room, Greg slowly walked over to the fireplace's mantelpiece. The six beautifully framed photographs told the story of a couple very much in love in a happy home. From left to right, Jeff shyly grinned at age ten. A family portrait of the three of them took up the next spot, then one of him in uniform, then Diane taken in the backyard, then one of Jeff and Diane when the boy was twelve. Finally, Jeff at his current age of twenty-two smiled for the camera. Jeff had Diane's warm blue eyes, friendly face, and exactly same smile.

Gently picking up Diane's photograph and holding it to his heart, tears rolled down Greg's cheeks. In this, another moment of unbearable sadness, he held it tighter, closed his eyes, clenched his lips and moved his head from side to side lamenting, "Oh, Darling … Oh, my dear, dear pal … I miss you so very much. At least you're at peace now, Sweetheart. No more suffering."

When Diane's favourite song finished, Greg placed the record in its sleeve, put it away and turned off the stereo. The words and delivery of Della Reece's beautiful recording had drained his body as it always did, and after wiping his eyes again, the detective knew he could not allow these emotions to get to him any longer. He knew he had to stop living in the past. Memories like this were wearing him down and taking over and he had fought the battle to the point where reason ought to prevail if it were given a chance. Besides, Diane wouldn't want him walking around like a vegetable.

With the song's significant meaning still etched on his mind, the newspaper's headlines captured Greg's attention. Establishing a disapproving look as he put on his glasses, he grumbled, "So, you son of a bitch, you're still at large, are you?"

MANIAC

Chapter 2

"Helen, where's that gorgeous daughter of yours?" Greg asked, adding, "You know, the movie star?"

Displaying a mother's knowing look, Helen Potts said, "You mean the movie star that always chews her nails and is boy crazy? Where else? She's either sitting at home waiting for Philip, or pasting another picture in her endangered birds' book. I swear if all the birds in the world flew in our backyard, Sandy would give them each a name and feed them. When she was young and we went anywhere, if a bird came along everything would be put on hold until it flew away."

"I'd say she's waiting for Philip," Jim Potts stated, agreeing with his wife right down to the contrived agitated look that jumped from her face to his.

"Yeah, why am I fooling myself?" Helen asked, offering an exasperating grin. "She's always waiting for Philip."

"Prince Philip?" Greg enquired, chuckling away. "With a body like Sandy's got, she could have all the princes and kings at her feet."

With no wind at ground level, it was hard not to imagine the swirling fury high above, dispersing clouds and letting the sun's warm rays dry everything out just in time for the Laidlaw pool party.

"Someone loves us," Wayne said, glancing at the blue sky while his wife tuned into a music station on the portable radio she had just brought out of the house.

The host and hostess wore chefs' hats, and as Wayne turned over steaks, Glenda served drinks, Joan Sumislouski smeared sunscreen on her twin six-year-old boys, and Larry splashed the crystal blue water while tossing Jim and Helen Potts' two younger girls one by one over his shoulders.

"Doctor Sumislouski tosses us higher than you do, Daddy," Merriam Potts happily declared, experiencing the point of weightlessness before falling into Larry's strong arms and being hurled upwards again. "This is fun, isn't it, Christine?"

The child's parents acknowledged their daughter's flight, and Jim said, "He's a dentist, Sweetie. Everything he does is higher … mainly his fees."

Larry laughed and spit some water at Jim. "I've got to be high priced just to pay off my golf bets. Wayne, this pool is great, but why did you build it at this time of year?"

Wayne Laidlaw flipped over another steak and took a swig from his bottle of Budweiser. "We figured if we held onto the money we'd just spend it. Probably a good portion of it with our dentist."

"Larry, you won today, so what are you complaining about?" Greg asked, sitting on the end of the diving board, agilely holding on to his can of beer while rolling up his pant-legs.

This time Larry tossed the other young Potts' girl, Christine, into the air. "And got accused of cheating," he said. "Just wait till the next time you guys have cavities."

"We're still paying off our last visit, so we hope it will be a while," Wayne said, seasoning the steaks. "If we keep getting your bills I might have to stop selling chemicals and rob a bank. Ain't that right, my dear?"

Placing her hands on her hips, Glenda gleefully replied, "You bet! Each time you check our teeth, we have to re-mortgage this joint."

"My fees are quite reasonable, thank you," Sumislouski said, splashing with the girls. "One of my ex colleges, Dr. Ogden Ellison, charges twice the going rate I charge, and gets away with it. Not once has he had a complaint. Now there's a dentist who knows exactly how long to keep his patients in his chairs. Right to the second."

"Well, you wouldn't find us going to him," Wayne said, visibly proud of the steaks he salted. "I don't mind paying a bit over the norm, but I don't want you to think you're a branch office of our bank."

As Larry Sumislouski laughed, his wife Joan stopped tickling one of her sons. When the boy ran off, she said, "We'll have to re-mortgage our house too if that car isn't finished soon."

Larry somehow managed to toss both girls high into the air at the same time. Splashing them when they landed, he said, "Honey, everyone needs a hobby. I can't help it if the Ford costs us more than I thought."

"How long have ya been working on it?" Greg asked, lifting his legs up and crossing them on the diving board rather than getting his pant legs soaked.

"Six months. Well, maybe six months seriously. When I bought it, I had to…"

"Fibber," said Joan. "I hardly ever see you. You've been at it for over a year. You're never away from Everton or some small town buying parts, and sometimes you're up until two in the morning. I'm just happy we had a shower constructed in the basement."

"Make that three in the morning," Jim Potts said. "I always give Larry a hand when I can, and one night we had one hell of a time putting in new rings. I had no sleep because

I had to go to work at three thirty. I should have charged you for that help, Doctor Sumislouski."

Larry merrily waved off Jim's comment and swam over to Joan. "Sweetheart, it sat in a farmer's field for over thirty-five years. Gimmee a break. You asked me to get a hobby."

"Must be full of manure," Wayne said. "Not you, Larry, the Ford."

"Grinning, Sumislouski declared, "It had grass growing everywhere ... even up through the floorboards. I'm still clearing it out. But hey, but have you seen how it's starting to look?"

"Tell me about it, Larry," Joan said, standing up and stretching. "I'm still cleaning mud out of our basement."

"So it's a dirty labour of love. Honey, it won't always be that way. I enjoy it, but I never knew parts for a '49 Ford were so expensive ... and tough to get."

As Glenda replaced Greg's beer, Greg said, "A year? Larry, you could have rebuilt that car six times over?"

"Greg, I'm a dentist, not a mechanic. I haven't repaired a car since I was eighteen. It took me two months just to scrape the dirt off the bottom and the wheel wells, but having a hobby is great. Do ya hear me, Greg Britton?"

Greg pretended he didn't hear the hint, and like most of them, he laughed when Joan said, "Darling, take up stamp collecting next time. It's a cleaner pastime. Either that or put a shower in the garage."

While Glenda Laidlaw searched her memory and rushed away muttering, "I've forgotten to bring out something. Ah, the potato salad," Larry said, "Anyway, the Ford's nearly finished. Anyone know a good car painter?"

"I'll paint it for you, cheap, Uncle Larry," little Christine Potts offered upon climbing out of the shimmering pool, and drying off by jumping up and down.

The child's father seized the moment for a wisecrack as he wrapped a towel around his daughter. "Not cheap, Darlin' ... we'll use his rate chart."

Larry indicated he enjoyed the witticism. "Thanks anyway, Sweetie. I'll remember your offer when I need something painted."

Greg felt thoroughly relaxed listening to the banter coming from the melting pot of personalities around him. The youngest of his friends, Doctor Larry Sumislouski and his wife Joan, hadn't lived in the neighbourhood long but it seemed like he had known them all his life. Both were intelligent, tall, good looking and athletic. Joan had taught school until the twins came along and she decided not to return to work. Larry had a busy dentistry practice and his main hobbies were jogging, golf, and recently a return to the devoted mechanics of hands-on car repairing. Britton thought they were a great couple, and super neighbours.

"How's your beer, Greg? Wayne asked, walking away after hearing "Good, thanks."

Greg Britton thought Wayne and Glenda were the perfect hosts. He really liked them. It always appeared the couple never took anything or anyone seriously, yet if people were in need or asked them for a hand or a favour, it was done instantly. As well, the duo always wore perpetual smiles that would take an atom bomb to erase.

Glenda Laidlaw had been Diane's best friend. Around the same age, the two always shopped, played golf and tennis, and lunched together at least once a week. Greg and Wayne couldn't spare that much time together. While Greg was out solving cases, Wayne drove all over the state selling chemicals. Still, because of their wives' relationship, the two men enjoyed each other's company and played golf whenever possible.

Glenda and Wayne had met in college and had travelled around the world before they bought their house next-door. The couple had two boys, Glen Junior, and Earl, and like their dad, the boys were sports mad and had won sports scholarships. Presently, young Glen served as an officer in the navy, and Earl scoured the country as a government geologist. Both boys were married with children, and as the boys grew up, Greg and Diane always filled the role of quasi grandparents.

"When Sandra Potts and her boyfriend Philip arrived, Wayne yelled, "I love your bikini, Sandy. Steaks are ready ... Glenda where's that salad?"

Sandra beamed. "Thanks, Mr. Laidlaw."

"That's what I forgot again. Coming up," Glenda said, walking briskly back into the house.

"That's a bikini?" Greg asked. "If that's a bikini, all the girls in Playboy Magazine are overdressed."

Sandra grinned shyly and Philip just looked awkwardly out of place putting two lawn chairs together and sitting down. When he first walked in, Sandra's boyfriend had smiled and nodded at Jim and Helen Potts, but like most parents raising girls, Jim just grunted and ignored the boy.

A knowing smile came to Greg Britton's lips watching Jim and Helen observe their eldest daughter. He admired them immensely and couldn't ask for better friends. Originally, after Sandra was born, the pair had said no more kids. Later, fully understanding the risk, they tried twice for a boy, but were more than happy when two healthy girls arrived.

Chuckling inwardly, Greg watched Jim and Helen Potts handle Philip. Many boys had preceded Philip, so the couple knew what to expect. They were the kind of people that would open their hearts and wallets to strangers. They kept their house spotless but by no means were they concerned with fancy furnishings and the like. Staying healthy and bringing up healthy kids was all that mattered.

The two Salvation Army members in their middle forties attended meetings regularly and took pride in spending as much time as possible assisting others. When Diane got sick, Helen Potts hardly ever left her side. Even with many home responsibilities or serving on the Salvation Army's Sick and Visiting Hospital Committee, Helen was always there to help Diane. As for Jim, Greg thought he was great; the kind of a person that should be presented with the President's Good

Citizen's Award. Balding like Greg, Jim Potts worked for American Customs, and when he wasn't at work, or at the temple, or helping pensioners and single fathers, or driving his three girls to various functions, he enjoyed being on the golf course with his neighbours. Jim and Helen each enjoyed having a few beers now and then, and Greg found that surprising considering the couple's loyalty to what they referred to as "God's Salvation Army. They usually only drank certain brands of non-alcoholic beer, but if those weren't available, normal alcoholic brands would suffice. The two weren't hypocrites; everything they did, they did in moderation, and that even included having the odd alcoholic beverage. He remembered once asking Jim if the Salvation Army allowed its members to drink alcohol, and Jim said, "Why not? Christ drank wine."

"You must be Philbert," Glenda Laidlaw asked, hastily shaking the muscular boy's right hand while on one of her trips to the kitchen. "Welcome to our humble abode."

The unsure teenager dressed in jeans with an unbuttoned sports shirt exposing his strapping upper body didn't respond, but he did nod, and Sandra laughed saying, "His name's Philip, and he's totally shy."

Although Philip turned a shade pink, he said, "Sandy, I'm not shy. You can totally bet I'm not shy."

Always one to 'stir up the pot' Greg climbed up from the end of the board, saying, "Shy? Hell, he's probably the strong silent type. Anyway, Philbert sounds better."

When their eyes calculatingly met, both males grinned.

"How's your drink, Greg?" Wayne asked again, before saying, "C'mon everyone, dig in. C'mon, you kids get over here and get your hotdogs."

"Still good, Wayne. I'll also have some of that wine when it gets here. Er ... did anyone see today's headlines?"

"About the rapist?" Jim Potts asked, standing behind Greg, sniffing the barbecue's aroma and holding out his plate.

"Yeah."

As Wayne heaped a steak on Greg's plate, Larry said, "The bastard's getting close. That last girl only lives six blocks away."

"How old is she?" the *chef* asked.

Greg helped himself to some potato salad. "Seventeen. Apparently two days earlier, she mentioned to her mother she thought she saw someone at her window."

"C'mon, you kids, there's pop here," Glenda said, returning from the house and offering wine around.

"At her window? When was this?" Larry asked.

The detective accepted a glass of wine. "Thanks, Kiddo. Er, two days before the S.O.B. entered the house at midnight and raped her."

"Didn't her parents tell the police about the window thing?" Jim Potts asked.

"Evidently not," Greg said, indicating he liked the chilled wine. "They thought she imagined it. Can you believe that?"

"Well that's number six around here," Sumislouski stated, displaying a concerned look. "The bastard is..." Quickly covering his mouth, Larry grinned at the children. "Sorry about that, kids. The S.O.B. is getting closer. We're so concerned, we've discussed installing a burglar alarm."

"What kind of parents must they be?" Glenda said, musing and shaking her head after sitting next to her husband. "A burglar alarm? That's a good idea."

"We've got double locks, and Ripper our dog patrols the house, Helen Potts advised."

"Helen, Ripper's hearing went years ago," Jim Potts said, grinning and pointing his fork at his wife. "He couldn't bite an intruder ... he'd have to gum the guy."

A smile slowly found its way across Greg's face. "Speaking of gumming and guarding, we've all got Madge."

Suddenly, Wayne stood in such a hurry his plate almost fell off his knee and most people thought he had just been stung. Staring at the Gosling place across the alley, he shouted, "Did anyone see that?"

"See what?" Greg asked, quickly turning his head and staring at the Gosling house, an exact duplicate of his own house but without a back porch.

Only a small portion of Wayne Laidlaw's astonishment had disappeared. "I just saw Ronnie Gosling standing naked at the window. At least I think it was Ronnie Gosling, it could have been the old man. It happened so fast, the second he saw me he closed the drapes. Jesus Christ, didn't any of you see that? He was holding a butcher knife."

"The Lord doesn't like his name used in that manner," Jim said softly.

Wayne glanced understandably at his friend. "Er, yes, I'm sorry."

"Who had a butcher knife?" Greg asked.

"Either Vernon or Ronnie Gosling had a massive butcher knife in his right hand."

All eyes that were immediately aimed at the Gosling house saw nothing but drawn drapes.

When their minds cleared, Jim Potts placed a daughter on each knee and held them tightly. "Greg, you said Ronnie was never found guilty. Why was that?"

"Well, I believe all the investigations were botched, and the man also always had alibis. As well, they did a DNA test on the last girl and the results clearly proved Gosling was not the killer."

"How were they botched?" Jim asked.

"Rookie investigative teams contaminating what evidence there was, and allowing far too much interfering foot traffic. Some people still believe Gosling's guilty though, and they think he had a partner."

"That's scary," Sumislouski said, exhibiting a concerned repulsive look while spurting some mustard on a hotdog and handing it to one of his boys. "Two creeps working with each other. How sick can people be?"

As the adults mulled over Greg's statements, Jim and Helen Potts didn't notice Sandy had untied her top before stretching out face down on the lawn. In a roundabout way, Wayne Laidlaw brought it to Jim's attention.

"The way Sandy is developing, I'd be concerned. You'll need double locks!"

Sandra cackled, saying, "Thank you Mr. Laidlaw. You're the first totally cool adult to notice I'm growing up."

"Sandy, what are you doing? Do up your top," Helen ordered, perturbed and embarrassed her daughter would do such a thing.

Before the teenage girl could obey, Wayne rushed over and after straddling her, tried to pick her up by her waist. "Growing up? If I was fifteen I'd be camping on your doorstep."

"Help! Stop it, I totally like it," Sandra yelled, holding her top tightly against her body.

"If you were camping on our doorstep, I'd have two shotguns above the door instead of one" Jim Potts humorously stated before turning his head and locking eyes with a grinning Philip, now swallowing and trying to hide a guilty look while casually looking away.

After tickling her sides and releasing the girl, Wayne headed back to his chair, but not before saying, "Are those bikinis legal? They look a lot like shoestrings."

Glenda gave her husband a penetrating stare. "Two grown up daughters and you talk like that? What's this world coming to?"

"Oh, settle down, Mother," Wayne said, getting up again and giving his wife a peck on her left cheek. "You don't talk like that when you invite ... er, beg me to get into your shower. Sandy is an extremely beautiful girl. It's all right if I pay you a compliment, isn't it, Sandy?"

Always grinning, but this time exhibiting a little abashment, Glenda jovially pushed Wayne away. "Wayne Laidlaw, how could you even...?"

Greg smiled, saying, "It's probably the other way 'round, right Glenda?"

"You bet it is. Every since we married, I've called him a sex maniac."

Wayne kissed his wife again. "Yeah, and the day you stop, you'll be bathing alone."

"Is that a promise?" Glenda asked.

Sandra's face also turned red, but her Scarlet O'Hara chin rose proudly when she nodded. "I totally wish all the boys would pay me those compliments, Mr. Laidlaw."

"You can totally bet I will always do that, Sandy, and..." Philip's eagerness abruptly ended and the boy slunk lower in his chair after receiving forewarning looks from Mr. and Mrs. Potts.

"Uh, Daddy, the girls on Bay Watch undo their tops when they tan."

"This ain't Bay Watch," Jim Potts sternly asserted before allowing everyone to witness his slight grin. "Remember, you're only fifteen."

"Fifteen, going on thirty," Helen added.

Watching the sun's rays dance off the water onto Sandy's bronzed body, Greg sensed the need to lighten up the conversation. "Don't worry, Honey, you've got lots of time to experience life. I'm certain all the boys notice you ... they're just shy, that's all."

Everyone laughed at Philip's saintly presumptuousness when he said, "You can totally bet I ain't never shy, am I Sandy?" A second later, that same laughter turned to howls when Jim responded by saying, "Then Son, you'd better get totally shy and pretty quick. And you can totally and certainly bet on that."

"Sandy, can you baby-sit tomorrow night?" Joan Sumislouski asked after indicating she had forgotten to ask earlier.

"Gee, I'd like to, but I'm babysitting for the Greenbergs. That reminds me, I was supposed to call them today to confirm I'll be there. I'll phone them later."

"Who's taking you there?" Jim asked, moving his eyes between Philip and Sandra.

"They're only about three blocks away, but Philip's driving me there, and he'll be bringing me home."

Always the cop, Greg asked, "How old are you, Phil?"

"Seventeen, sir."

The police officer smiled. "Great age."

Without looking at Philip, Jim Potts said, "Well, if he doesn't drive you home, you phone and I'll...."

"Oh, Daddy, you're such a worrywart. Philip will have me home by eleven. Isn't that right, Philip?"

Under the omniscient eyes of Jim and Helen Potts, the male teenager swallowed hard before motioning he'd be doing the driving. "You can totally bet I will."

For some reason Greg Britton felt more secure entering his house after the pool party. He'd had a good time with some wonderful friends, and he had been the last to leave. Not that he had far to go home, he thought, happily whistling and doing a bit of a jig while feeding Mickey.

The detective didn't know, nor did he care why he opened the liquor cabinet and took out a bottle of Lemon Heart rum. The action wasn't automatic - he hadn't touched his bar in over six months, but now he felt contented and wanted a drink. This was the first night since Diane's death he didn't feel alone. The hall clock wasn't resonating like the town square clock and the house gave him room - it wasn't crowding in on him tonight. He could think freely again, and as he sat at the kitchen table, Mickey jumped on his lap and the detective mentally analyzed the afternoon's activities. He was glad his son Jeff was well past the clumsy teenager stage, and not like Philip Bayer. Sandy's boyfriend seemed like a nice boy that could do no harm, but Greg remembered what it was like being a teenager. The parents of all the girls he went with also thought he could do no harm. After a belt of rum, he grinned mumbling, "No harm? Jesus, when I was seventeen, no harm meant no girl was safe."

It didn't take Greg long to finish his drink and pour another. Sitting down again, he recalled Helen saying Sandy was fifteen going on thirty. "Boy is Helen ever right," he mumbled. "Sandy really is beautiful. A beautiful girl in a neighbourhood with a maniac on the loose."

Just as the party ended, Greg remembered Helen saying, "Even with double locks and Ripper, I'm scared when Jim leaves the house at three-thirty each morning. Greg why can't they catch the guy?"

"They will, Helen. I've got a feeling he lives around here."

"Around here?" Sumislouski asked, displaying the same concern as his wife Joan. "That's all we need. How do you figure that?"

"He knows the streets. Our cars grid the area minutes after he leaves his victims, yet he still vanishes."

Sumislouski offered, "Since he's back at it, maybe we should organize ourselves and start a real Block Watch program?"

"Larry, police cars are circling our block every fifteen minutes now," Britton stated, displaying a slightly frustrated look. "I know you're worried because you've got kids, but the little old ladies are nervous too. We'll get him."

"Why hasn't anyone recognized him?" Glenda asked.

Larry wiped mustard off both boys' faces. "They can't. The newspapers say the S.O.B. wears a blue woollen hood."

"You miss the force, don't you, Greg?" Jim Potts asked, wobbling over and sitting beside his friend. "You said, 'We'll get him.'"

A nostalgic grin took control of Greg's lips. "Did I say that, Jimmy, old buddy? I guess I did. It's just habit, Jim, but it's only a matter of time before we get our hands on him."

When Christine Potts said, "Maybe he's a werewolf, Uncle Larry?" Sumislouski gently took hold of the child's hand. "No, he's not a werewolf, Precious. He's a head case that needs to be put away. And the sooner, the better."

By the time Greg Britton finished his second drink, he'd stopped recollecting and his head told him it was time for bed. He had really enjoyed this day. After pulling the bedclothes up to his chin and rolling over on his left side and closing his eyes, the policeman grinned thinking of the looks on certain faces when Wayne Laidlaw said, "Okay, you kids, I have hidden quarters all over the yard. After you finish eating, you can search for 'em."

"Hey, you can totally bet we will," a *kid* with a deep voice replied.

"Hold it, hold it. Not you, Philip. I said 'kids'. Please be seated."

For some reason, attending the barbecue had exhausted Greg Britton. As his snores competed with the incessant ticking of his grandfather clock, two houses away, a lone figure stood outside Sandra Potts' brightly lit bedroom window.

Normally the intruder always assumed a crouching position outside the window, but earlier Sandra had opened it along with her curtains. The man did not like viewing the girl from a higher angle, and with the window remaining open, he knew he must be extremely quiet.

Although he wore dark clothing, the stranger realized if he stood in front of the window, his body would interrupt the room's light shining on the fence and the girl would see his silhouette. No, he would have to stay completely to the side and bring his head back as she came near.

With her hair wrapped in a towel, Sandra hummed along with her radio as she removed her bathrobe, threw it on a chair, and searched a drawer for baby-doll pyjamas. When she found the items, she didn't put them on right away - instead, she picked up the telephone.

"Hello, Mr. Greenberg, it's Sandy. I'm sorry I didn't call you earlier, but I attended a pool party. What's that? That's right ... at Mr. and Mrs. Laidlaw's. Yes, they are totally nice people. Uh, what time do you want me over there tomorrow night? Yes, seven until midnight's fine. No, that's not necessary - my boyfriend will drop me off and pick me up. Okay, thanks Mr. Greenberg. Good night."

The overwhelming silky-smooth beauty of the naked teenage girl's skin was almost too much for the trespasser. In his excitement, he moved his right foot and it scraped a small pebble on the cement path. To him, the stone's action sounded like a thousand exploding cannons rupturing his ears and he immediately moved away. Inside the house though, Sandra's radio dulled the noise. Still, she thought she heard something and rushed to her window, closed it and pulled her curtains together.

As soon as the girl walked away from the curtains, the intruder's lips formed an evil grin. The girl's curtains had been washed so many times when she pulled them together they separated slightly. This allowed the man to crouch and view his *trophy* at eye level.

Sandra also didn't put on her baby-dolls after she finished speaking with Mr. Greenberg. Instead, the well-proportioned naked girl reclined on her bed writing in her diary. When finished, she tucked the book under her mattress, took out a teenage magazine, walked to her dresser and assumed the same posing positions of her favourite stars.

Had Sandra's window remained open, she would have heard the guttural moans of ecstasy her pursuer released while he visualized caressing her attractively sculptured breasts and stroking her glistening hair.

When the girl sauntered elegantly to her bed to lie on her stomach, the predator's eyes explored the nape of her neck joining her faultless back and her determined but gently curved goddess-like buttocks. Just the elegant movements of the stunning girl forced the invader to place his head in his hands and groan loudly while repeatedly ejaculating in his pants like an erupting volcano.

With his mind raging, the intruder wanted to rip off his clothes and his skin, fill his lungs with fresh air and release thunderous screams of frustration and failure into the night. No, he would not allow this bitch to control him any longer. This whore. This impure immoral wench. This filthy fucking slut taunting him and dominating his every thought seven days a week had to die. I'll have her shortly, he thought, licking his lips. Oh yes, yes, yes, I'll have her. I'll invade every one of her orifices at will - even the new ones she'll have when I carve her open. Should I take her now? I could. Fuckin' right I could. She's lyin' on her back steadily opening and closing her legs before cupping them up to her tits and baring her pudenda for me. She's doin' it for me; I know she is. Nah, I'll let her live a little longer. I heard her conversation with Greenberg and I know exactly where...

The trespasser stopped pondering and froze, as a spotlight appeared slowly advancing down the alley. Instantly, he saw Madge's curtains move and at that exact same moment, he heard tire squeals in front of the Potts' house.

That goddamned old bitch has called the cops again. I'll get her too. I'll cut that nosy fucking hag. I should have done her in before now. Fuck, why wasn't I warned?

As his heart picked up the beat, the intruder's hands began shaking uncontrollably and the right side of his face twitched violently. What to do? If he went towards the front yard, he would be caught, and the police would capture him if he ran into the alley.

The hooded man only had seconds to make up his mind and he knew there was only one direction to go. Placing both hands on the top of the fence, he jumped allowing his upward motion to take him up and over the wooden barrier into Larry and Joan Sumislouski's yard. Now he had to run swiftly and hide, hoping the police hadn't brought in their dogs.

The police car shined its spotlight in all yards as it made its way down the alley, finally stopping at Madge's house on the east side of the lane across from Jim and Helen's house.

Holding her hands in front of her eyes, the old woman walked out onto her back porch. "It's about time!"

"Are you the person who called us?" the lone police officer asked while stepping out of his car.

"I don't drink gin. Never have liked the stuff. All the boys' called it panty remover, so I left it alone. I've lived here for forty years," Madge replied, cupping her right ear. "In this same house. I don't even smoke anymore. I can't see you … turn off your light."

The police officer switched off his spotlight and yelled, "No, no, no. I asked if you are the person that telephoned? Are you Mrs. Grant?" he asked, watching the stocky grey-haired woman standing on her back porch and holding the front of her dressing gown together to keep out the wind.

"I usually don't wear pants - they're not ladylike. I feel fine in a woollen skirt and sweater, but right now, this dressing gown is adequate. I bought it in…"

A sour look gripped the police officer. "No, no, lady. Did you telephone us?"

"Yes, it was me," Madge said, dressed only in slippers, her nightgown and the dressing gown she was about to describe. Visibly uncomfortable in the night air, she added, "I thought I saw someone at Sandra's window again."

"Again?" the cop asked.

"What? Speak up, I'm in my seventies, you know."

"You said, 'Again?'"

"Yes, there was someone there last night as well."

Speaking a little louder but trying to keep his voice down because of the time, the officer said, "No one told us about that. Can you come here, please?"

"No, you meet me half way."

Normally Madge Grant never made many mistakes. The widowed pensioner had the unique knack of foretelling predicaments before they happened. On this night, however, with a police officer so close to her house, Madge felt over secure and left her back door open while she spoke with the officer.

"You say this occurred last night as well?" the police officer asked while making notes.

"What occurred?" Madge asked.

"You said you thought you saw a man in that yard."

"Well, yes, I think so. My eyes aren't the best, but I could have sworn I saw the gate open and someone in the yard. You won't be able to see so well either when you're my age."

"Did you recognize the person?"

"What person. Please be specific, officer."

"The person in the yard,"

"Not really. He crouched by the fence."

"What time was that?"

Looking at her watch, Madge asked, "You want the time?"

"No, no, not the time right now. The time you thought you saw someone in that yard?"

"About ten-thirty. This morning I mentioned it to Dr. Sumislouski who lives right there, next door, and he said he'd speak with Mr. Potts."

The cop made notes as she spoke. "Did he?"

"Did he what? I'm not a mind reader, you know?"

"Did he speak with Dr. Sum ...er, did Dr. Sumislouski speak with Mr. Potts?"

"I don't know. How the hell would I know?"

"Do you think Dr. Sumislouski will still be up?"

"Up where? He's not a climber he's a dentist. Listen, Sonny, get your brain in gear. I'm old enough to burp you and you look like you need to be burped."

Tapping his toe didn't help the officer. "No, no, I mean ... do you think he's gone to bed?"

"How the hell would I know if he's in bed? That's a little personal isn't it? I would think so; there doesn't appear to be any lights on in his house. Any idiot can see that."

Intuition told the police officer he was speaking to a busybody of the worst kind but her actions were somewhat cute. Still, he had to follow through with his investigation even if the old biddy was imagining things.

"Well, let me ask you a question, Mrs. Grant. I drove down this alley and another squad car is parked out front of the Potts house ... how do you think the man got out of the yard?"

"What man?" Madge asked.

"The man you said you saw in the yard."

"I don't know, young man. When I saw your car, I left the window and came to open my door. He must have moved then. Yeah, that's right. I saw him jump over the fence."

Frustration showed on the cop's face. "I know that, Mrs. Grant, but where did he go?"

"Who?"

"The man in the yard."

"How the hell do I know where he went ... you're the policeman? He went into Doctor Sumislouski's yard. You should have caught this rapist long ago. If my Horace was alive he'd have caught him."

"Ah, so your husband was a member of our force?"

"I didn't say that. He was an undertaker."

Quizzed, the officer asked, "Then how would Horace have caught him?"

"How did you know my husband's name was Horace? Did you know him?"

"No, I never had the pleasure. You just told me."

Madge tightly held the front of her dressing gown and turned back to her house. "I did? Well, it's too cold out here, I'm going in."

"You didn't answer me."

Turning, she asked, "I'm sorry, what was your question?"

"How could Horace have caught him?"

"Horace would have got hold of one of his fishing bonkers and gone over there and bonked the bastard on the head. That's what you should have done. Good night to you, Officer."

Upon re-entering her house, Madge shivered slightly and double locked her back door. Although she spent more time at her dining room window, the television remained on in her living room and she went in to turn it off. Upon entering the dark hallway, she heard a strange bumping sound coming from her bedroom.

Slowly walking toward her bedroom's closet door, Madge Grant never knew how close she came to having a bread knife slice through her neck. A persistent push on her front door's buzzer turned the old woman around and saved her life. Heading to answer the door, she said, "If that goddamned tomcat is in my closet again, I'll castrate the bastard. Hold on, hold on, I'm coming. Who the hell is it now?"

When Madge opened the door, the same police officer wearing the same questioning look stood there with the same notebook in hand. "Er, Mrs. Grant, sorry to bother you again."

"That's all right."

"How tall would you say he is?"

When Madge asked, "Who?" the officer became further perplexed. "Who? The intruder of course; who else would I be talking about?"

Madge thought for a moment. "Don't get facetious with me, young fellow; I meant, which one?"

Quickly glancing up from his notebook, the police officer became puzzled. "You mean you've seen more than one man at that window?"

"Yes, I think so, but I can't tell for sure 'cause they crouch down. Only one of them wears a hood."

"You mean they're together?"

"No, they're always alone. At least I think they're alone. One's about six feet or a little more, and the other one's a few inches smaller."

"And their weight?" the police officer asked.

"Both about 180 or 200 pounds."

After the police officer left, Madge muttered to herself making her final rounds before going to bed. "I thought I had already locked that," she said, hesitating at the back door trying to search her memory. A few seconds later after shaking off the notion, the senior double locked the back door *again* and turned out her kitchen light.

Chapter 3

At ten-fifteen on Sunday morning, Greg Britton crossed the alley behind his house and after opening the Goslings' gate, he couldn't believe the state of their yard. Obviously, the two men had been growing their own vegetables because every square foot of the once beautiful lawn had been dug up to plant all types of vegetables. Now after wading through rotten cabbages, potatoes, cornhusks, overgrown grass, weeds and garbage bags full of fresh soil and clay, leaves and trash, the police officer climbed the creaky back stairs and knocked on the door of the rundown house. Greg was aware the same contractor that had built his residence had built the Gosling house, but by the look of the dump, he found it hard to believe.

No one came to the door at first, but Britton heard movement inside and after pounding again, four locks and bolts unlatched and the door opened three inches, held by additional chain locks.

"Yeah? What do you want?" a slurred but direct voice asked.

Even through the slit, Greg recognized Vernon Gosling's hazel eyes – one normal and the left one-half closed due to a thyroid problem the man had in his twenties. He had grey hair and a bony unshaven face. Although the lieutenant hadn't seen Gosling for a while, he remembered him well. The man was strong without an ounce of fat, and extremely agile. Most people at his age physically slowed down a little, but not Vernon Gosling. He could run ten miles without breaking a sweat, and rumour had it he could squeeze a beer bottle with one hand until it cracked.

Greg wasn't prepared for the abundantly stained nicotine fingers with filthy fingernails wrapped around the door edge or the putrid musty odour now assailing his nostrils. He thought the man's personal habits must have changed completely. "Do you remember who I am, Vern?"

When Gosling curtly answered, "I said, what do you want?" the detective noticed the man's voice had turned throaty.

"May I come in?"

"No."

"Is your son, Ronnie, in?"

"Yes."

"Did he go out last night?"

"No. But if he did, it's not your fuckin' business."

Although Greg couldn't quite get a full view of Gosling's face, he thought what a difference eight years had made. At one time, the half-naked hermit hiding behind the door had been outgoing and friendly. He would laugh and tell jokes over the fence, and even help Madge and other neighbours with their shopping and tasks. Gosling's wife had died giving birth to their son Ronald, and the old man was proud of the fact his son had become a medical doctor, and then a world famous heart surgeon.

Gosling didn't have to live the life of a cheap hermit. Greg knew Vernon Gosling had sections of farmland all over

Northern Washington which he leased or hired farmers to plant various vegetables. Gosling would take off for months at a time to reap the benefits his land provided, and that's how he put Ronald through university. Now he locked himself away like his boy and people called them the "Howard Hughes duo."

It all started after a thorough investigation in Everton, Washington, when police officers charged Dr. Ronald Gosling, then a prominent heart surgeon, with killing two female patients and raping four others. For three years, Gosling had been going mad but had managed to hide his condition from his family, patients, and fellow professionals. Following a prolonged trial with a hung jury that tried but couldn't get one educated answer from Dr. Ronald Gosling, the experts certified him mentally incapable of killing. The jury thought that perhaps Doctor Gosling exhibited the 'Dr. Jekyll and Mr. Hyde' syndrome. At the height of his young career, a second character unlike his own began to take control of his mind. At first, the other man only took up a few seconds of Dr. Gosling's character, but bit-by-bit that scenario changed as the new personality took complete and total control of the doctor. He was sentenced to life in a sanatorium but after two years, a review board consisting of various bureaucrats, psychiatrists and psychologists found him non-threatening and approved his release into the custodianship of his father. Only after his discharge did various police officials consider Dr. Gosling a suspect in a multitude of unsolved rapes and killings in cities and towns in Northern Washington State. No charges were ever laid because the medical professional always had alibis and the macabre crime scenes were bare of incriminating evidence.

"Does Ronnie ever go out?" Greg asked.

"No, I won't let him, and he doesn't want to go anyway. Listen, what's that got to do with you? Just what the fuck do you want, Britton?"

"How do you control Ronnie when you leave the house?"

"That's my business."

"Ronnie stood naked with a butcher-knife in his hand at that window yesterday," Greg said, pointing to the house's back window. "I want to know why?"

"He was killin' a mosquito."

"With no clothes on and a butcher-knife in his hand?"

When the elder Gosling's lips opened and his mouth curled into a malicious grin, Greg witnessed a mouthful of yellow-stained teeth.

"You know Ronald has his own peculiar little ways of doing things, Britton," Gosling said, flippantly. "His action didn't bother anyone other than giving the barbecue broads a thrill. Let's leave it at that. Anything else?"

"There were children present, Vernon."

Gosling obviously wasn't interested in whatever Greg had to say. He just grinned and cocked his head while mouthing, "Ask me if I give a fuck. I said, is there anything else?"

"Yeah, as a matter of fact. There have been a few murders and a series of rapes in this…"

Greg stopped conversing when Gosling yelled, "Fuck off!" and slammed the door in his face. Banging on it again did not gain Gosling's attention.

That Sunday evening, black clouds with accompanying winds came spewing in from the Pacific Ocean. Local residents knew they would last well into the night. As sheets of endless rain violated Harvey and Barbara Greenberg's wide porch and front room window, Sandra and Philip embraced and kissed on the couch.

The Greenbergs didn't believe it was healthy for young teens to be in their home without a chaperone and they had left explicit instructions that Philip was not to enter their house. Earlier, Sandra had agreed, but after the two children were asleep and her boyfriend phoned, Sandra gave in to the boy's persistent coaxing. With the lights low, the lovebirds kissed passionately and Sandra allowed Philip's right hand to remain up her sweater, gently fondling her breasts. Only when the boy tried to place a hand between her legs, did

Sandra back her lips off and push him away, whispering, "No, Phil ... I told you, no."

Philip alluringly kissed her again pleading, "Aw, c'mon, Babe? You know I love you?"

About the same time as Sandra stood up fixing her hair and saying, "I said, no! I'm not ready," a hooded man, drenched to his skin and protected from street view by the front of the porch briskly left the window, quietly crawled to the stairs, then after bounding down and running behind the house, vanished into the rainy night.

"God, what time is it?" Sandra asked, excitedly.

Philip checked his watch. "It's only nine-thirty - why?"

The girl hastily fastened her brassiere and began combing her hair. "You've got to leave, Phil. If the Greenbergs come home early, they'll be totally upset."

Lazily and not wanting to comply, Philip stood, straightened his clothing and headed for the door. In a discontented manner, he asked, "What time should I come back?"

"They said they'd be home at midnight, so be back by eleven-forty-five ... okay?"

"Sandy, it's only nine-thirty."

"I know, but they've come home early before. Besides, I'm working on next week's Statue of Liberty assignment."

That night, the Greenbergs arrived home just after midnight. They drove past at twelve-fifteen, recognizing and waving to Philip Bayer sitting behind the wheel of his 1976 silver Chevrolet Impala with its engine running and windshield wipers moving.

Seconds later Harvey Greenberg opened the door from the inside and Sandra appeared on the porch. "Thanks, Mr. Greenberg. Do you need me next Wednesday?"

"C'mon, Sandy," Philip yelled, exhibiting an exasperated look after rolling down his window.

Harvey Greenberg smiled paternally and walked the girl to the top of his steps. "You bet, Sandy. Can you be here at seven?"

Philip had his own agenda. "Sandy, I'm getting soaked. Hurry it up, will ya, please?"

Sandra angrily turned towards her boyfriend. "Listen, Philip Bayer, roll up your window and totally hold your horses why don'tcha!" Returning her attention to Harvey Greenberg, she said, "Sure Mr. Greenberg. How many hours?"

"Five. We'll be home at midnight."

Just as Sandra started walking down the stairs, Barbara Greenberg came to the front door. "Harv, Sandra's homework is here."

"Are you coming or not?" Philip yelled.

"Hold on, Sandy, you've forgotten your homework," Greenberg reminded her before heading inside. Moments later, he returned to the porch and handed the girl her books. "So it's Wednesday at seven - okay, Sandy?"

"Totally cool. I'll be here, Mr. Greenberg." Sandra said, walking down the stairs. "Goodnight."

"Goodnight, Sandy. Thanks a lot."

Sandy's babysitting employer didn't enter his house right away. The attitude of the girl's boyfriend bothered him so he decided to wait on the porch until the couple drove away.

"It's about time," Philip mouthed, now standing at the end of Greenberg's pathway.

When Sandra reached him, she said, "God, you're impatient. What's with you tonight?"

Philip walked Sandra to his car and opened the driver's door so she could enter and slide over on the bench seat.

"I'm sick of waitin' for ya … that's what's with me. I've been twiddling my thumbs since nine-thirty and you said to be here before midnight."

Sandra didn't get in. Thoroughly upset, she stomped away, saying, "Oh, sure … and I'm supposed to jump every time you snap your fingers? Take a hike … I'll walk."

Running ahead and standing in front of her, Philip took hold of his girl's left arm. "No you won't. Get in the car, Sandy!"

As Sandra shook off the boy's hand and loudly said, "Let go of me," lights came on in the hallway of the house to the left of the Greenbergs, and Harvey Greenberg stepped to the edge of his stairs. "Sandra, would you like me to drive you home?"

For some reason, Philip's grin jumped to his girlfriend's lips. "No thanks, I'm all right," she replied. "It's only a few blocks, and this guy is a total jerk at times."

Harold Greenberg was not the only person watching the teens hugging and confiding their innermost thoughts about their relationship and walking hand in hand back to their car. One block away, another man holding powerful binoculars appeared quite irritated the two teens had patched things up. He'd observed their body language during their argumentative discourse and the excitement aroused him greatly. Still, he knew it didn't matter what the teens did, he knew in minutes she would be his.

"I'm soaked," Philip said, turning up the car's radio.

"Well, you did it to yourself," Sandra replied, being a bit huffy again. "Only idiots would stand in this rain. Also, don't get mad at me because you had to leave your pool game early."

"How did you know I went to play pool?"

"Where else would you go? I know you like a book."

Philip took hold of Sandra's left hand and kissed it. "I'm sorry, Babe."

"You should be. At times, you're a total louse, Philip Bayer. The Greenbergs must think I go out with some sort of a nut."

"I really am sorry," Philip said, wincing and placing the inside of his right thumb to his mouth.

Sandra noticed her boyfriend's discomfort and asked, "What wrong with your thumb?"

"I cut it on a pop machine at the pool hall."

"You're just not with it tonight, are you?"

Philip tenderly pulled his girl closer, kissed her left cheek and wrapped her in his arms. "You bet. I'm never really with it when I'm near you."

"Mr. Greenberg gave me a two buck tip. They're a totally nice family."

A mischievous smile captured the boy when he slowly pulled away. "Sandy, er ... can we park outside your place for awhile?"

"I'd like to, but it's getting really late."

"Aw, c'mon, Sandy? I haven't seen you since nine-thirty."

"Well, okay, but only for a few minutes."

Grinning widely, Philip kissed his girl's left hand again. "I think you're ... what the hell? I think I've got a flat?"

"How do you know?" Sandra asked.

"I'm wobbling all over the road."

After pulling over and getting out, Philip's irritated face indicated a problem with his left front tire.

"What's wrong?" Sandra asked, sliding over to the driver's window.

"The fucking thing's flat," her boyfriend said, leaning in and turning off the ignition before taking the keys. "I hope my spare's okay," he added, opening the trunk and taking out his tire wrench, jack and spare tire. "Yeah, it is, thank God."

Every time Sandra opened the window, rain blew in. "Can ya fix it?" she asked.

Philip wiped the rain off his face and shook out his hair while jacking up the car. "Yeah, but I'm gettin' soaked."

Sandra could see her boyfriend's frustration and she didn't want to be late getting home. "Phil, I think I'd better walk. It's only two blocks."

Philip stood and stretched his back. "What, in this weather? Are you nuts? This won't take me long. Hang tight and I'll drive you."

The girl had already made up her mind. Opening the driver's door and getting out, she said, "I don't wanna be late."

"You might be a few minutes late, but at least you'll be dry."

Sandra reached in, got her books, and shut the door. "Call me tomorrow."

"Jeez, and you call me stubborn," Philip said, having difficulty getting a tire-nut loose. "You'll be soaked by the time you get home," he groaned, wiping the rain from his face.

"Are you gonna call me, or not?"

"Okay, okay, I'll call you. Don't I always?"

For some strange reason, rain has a tendency to pick up when it catches people without umbrellas, Sandra thought, wishing she had brought an umbrella or a raincoat. The downpour did what she suspected, and holding her books over her head didn't really help as the teen's fast walking pace turned into a brisk jog until she neared the alley and the back gate of her house.

A quivering male figure watching Sandra held his butcher knife tighter as the girl approached her gate. Purposefully running his thumb and a part of the palm of his hand over the blade's sharp edge and cutting himself badly, the man's savouring grin grew as blood streamed off his hand onto the ground. Pain was not part of his makeup where Sandra was concerned. Whenever he saw her, his agonizing sensation didn't allow pain to exist. Rather, cutting himself felt pleasurable, like his feelings for the beautiful teenager.

Seeing the backdoor light brought a grateful homecoming smile to Sandra's face before she wiped the rain from her eyes and reached over to unlatch the entrance to her backyard. The kitchen light remained on and the girl felt appreciative knowing her dad was waiting up for her, probably watching television. She knew he would ask her what took her so long while preparing a cup of hot chocolate she would take to the cosy comfort of her room.

Sandra Potts never got the chance to drink the warm liquid. Before she touched the gate's latch, two powerful hands grabbed her from behind.

Nearly fainting from the initial shock of the attack, Sandra dropped her books and fought fiercely trying to free herself from her attacker's uncompromising strength clenching her like a vice and forcing a chemical-drenched cloth over her mouth and nose.

Frantically shaking her head like dogs do when they try to hold on to a rope or rip a cloth apart didn't deter the attacker. She couldn't scream and he pressed his hand so hard she felt the pain of a finger partially pierce her left eye, break her nose, and impale some of her teeth on her tongue.

In her plight, the trembling girl remembered all the self-defence moves her father had taught her, to no avail. When she raked her malodorous attacker's legs, her footwear was too soft to be effective. Even lifting her feet off the ground and dropping her body didn't work; her assailant's intense single mindedness and powerful arms easily held her upright.

As the aggressor's hand pressed even harder on her face, vomit filled her mouth and she began retching as it burned her throat and gushed without exit at her lips and nose. The girl wanted to cough but couldn't and during the vicious struggle she knew she would drown in her own stomach contents or die from asphyxiation.

While her head spun wildly and a dark watery film spread over her eyes, the frightened girl watched the blurred slow motion image of her dad entering the kitchen and opening the fridge door. Now oblivious to her reeking attacker's guttural panting, young Sandra Potts fell limp, unaware she had peed herself.

His throat felt dry, but other than that, Greg Britton had no idea why he opened his eyes at two o'clock in the morning, sat up, put his feet on the floor.

A second later though when his mind cleared, the detective knew it was the light - a flashing red light fighting its way through his closed bedroom window drapes.

Standing at the window and yawning, Greg witnessed rain bouncing off a police ghost car pulling up behind an empty but lit up black and white police car in front of Jim and Helen Potts' house.

"I wonder what the hell's going on in there?" he murmured. "What could be wrong?"

After having a quick wash and getting dressed, Greg ran a comb through his hair. "Maybe Sandra and Philip have been in a traffic accident. Yeah, that's probably what has happened. Hope they're okay."

After nearly stepping on Mickey curled up by the base of the grandfather clock, the police officer grabbed his keys, slipped into a pair of loafers and a windbreaker and left his house through the front door. Flipping up his collar and closing the gate, he grimaced thinking the rain couldn't come down any faster as he watched two officers from another ghost car rush into the Potts' home.

The lieutenant didn't knock on the old house's weather-beaten front door. It was already open an inch, and when he entered, he winked at the worried faces of Merriam and Christine Potts wearing pyjamas and sitting halfway up the hallway stairs.

Making his way towards the kitchen, he could hear the disconsolate voices of Jim and Helen Potts talking with the police. Particularly Helen's pleading voice. "No, Sandy has never done this before. She knows she has to call us if she wants to stay out longer."

"My wife's right," Jim said. "Sandra's a good girl. Listen, we've told you ten times she wouldn't do this. She always comes home on time."

A couple of tired-looking plainclothesmen nodded to Greg on their way out, and the lieutenant acknowledged he had seen them before, but as uniformed officers.

"What's happened?" Greg asked, entering the kitchen and seeing his solemn-faced friends.

Sandra's anxious father stood at the stove making coffee while Helen sat red-eyed at the kitchen table, shakily kneading a Kleenex through her fingers. When she saw Greg, her eyes welled up as she stood and sat down again. "Oh, Greg … Sandra hasn't come home."

The lieutenant knew the two detectives, Allan Dabbit and Mel Holmes, standing at the back of the room by the door, but he didn't know the two uniformed police officers talking with Dabbit.

Holmes had the telephone tucked between his right cheek and shoulder and wrote into a notebook he held against a wall. When he hung up, all three detectives indicated they knew each other.

"Home from where?" Greg asked, joining Helen at the table.

"Harvey and Barbara Greenberg's place, where she was babysitting. Oh, Greg, where do you think she could be?"

"I phoned the Greenbergs," Jim said, pouring six coffees. "Sandra left just after midnight."

Greg accepted a coffee and asked, "I thought her boyfriend, Philip, was driving her home?"

"Mr. Greenberg said Philip picked Sandra up, and she and the boy had quite the argument," Jim said, placing the coffee pot back on the stove.

"Finish your coffees and join the others checking the neighbourhood," Dabbit told the uniformed police officers.

Watching Helen's shaking hands and her husband's restlessness, Greg knew the sad affair was taking a huge toll on Jim and Helen. "I'm sure everything will be all right," he said, trying to comfort them. "Uh, where's Philip now?"

"Not home," Holmes said, lighting up a smoke. We've put out an APB."

Both uniformed police officers placed their cups in the sink and left as Greg asked, "Jim, what time did you call the police?"

"We got the call at twelve-forty five" Detective Dabbit replied. "Seven units are covering the area, Lieutenant."

At that moment, Wayne and Glenda Laidlaw and Larry Sumislouski entered the kitchen through the front hallway.

All three appeared tired and it was obvious they had just tossed on their clothes.

"What the hell's going on?" Larry asked, his face displaying a compassionate concerned look. "What's wrong? Why didn't you call us?"

Glenda rushed over and placed her right arm around Helen's shoulders. "Did someone get hurt? What's the matter, Helen?"

Greg said, "Sandra's missing after babysitting."

Wayne accepted a coffee from Jim. "She's probably with her boyfriend. Didn't he say he'd pick her up?"

"Philip did pick her up, but they had a falling out, and now he's not home either," Jim Potts said, not knowing what to do with his hands or his body for that matter.

"They probably parked and fell asleep," Larry said, pulling out a chair and sitting down. "Don't worry, if he's with her she'll be fine."

Placing a hand over one of Glenda's hands, Helen said, "Sandra wouldn't do that. Glenda, will you check on Merriam and Christine while we stay near the phone?"

"You poor dear, you bet I will," Glenda Laidlaw replied, trying to look and do everything rational just to ease the anxiety in the room.

Detective Dabbit took a two-way radio out of his raincoat's right pocket and after adjusting a few switches, said, "Detectives One-Seven. Missing girl could be in a 1976 silver Chevy Impala, licence number EGR 449. The vehicle is registered to Philip Bayer, age seventeen, 1774 Carson Street, and was last seen at 2290 Spruce Brook Road. Check sections fourteen to nineteen and place three units in area twelve."

A female voice saying, "Ten-four, Detectives One-Seven," was followed by a squelch noise as the police officer placed the device on the kitchen table.

Sympathetic conversation engulfed the room until Detective Holmes cleared his throat while glancing at Greg. "Er, Lieutenant Britton, uh, I think it would be better if, er..."

Greg understood and nodded, knowing the officer wanted to question Sandra's parents without neighbours being present. "Sure. Er, Larry, Wayne, let's get dressed and look around." Looking compassionately at Jim and Helen, he asked, "Are you two okay?"

Jim managed an anxious grin. "Thanks guys, you're the best friends anyone could want to have."

Helen didn't know why, but she found herself picking up Sandy's photograph and showing it to Greg, as if to remind him what her daughter looked like. With her voice breaking and nearly inaudible, she desperately searched for answers, pleading, "Greg, you … you don't think she's been … that maniac's still…? Sandy's just … just a baby. She's so young and she's never…"

Shaking his head and wrapping her in his arms, Greg said, "Sweetheart, don't start thinking the worst. Right now, the two of you must be strong. I'm sure everything is going to be fine."

Helen's lost moist eyes scrutinized the lieutenant's face searching for even the slightest sign of scepticism that wasn't evident. The distressed mother had to know the truth, and she knew Greg was the kind of man that would step into the bullring with her family.

Empathetic defiance filled Greg's face as he lightly kissed Helen's forehead and gently whispered, "Helen, I know what the two of you are going through, and it's hell. Ease your mind, my dear; we'll get Sandy back home."

Detective Holmes didn't wait for the three friends to leave. Flipping the worn-out pages of his notebook, he said, "Now, let's start from the beginning. What was she wearing?"

Jim Potts almost didn't hear the question. While pacing, every memory of Sandra growing up entered his mind. She was a quiet baby that never bothered anyone. There were times when she fell a little behind in school, but she made up for those times and received above average marks in all subjects. Focusing on the detective, Jim Potts said, "White jeans … yes, white jeans, a white sweater, blue windbreaker, and white deck runners." That said, he continued pacing back and forth again. He couldn't even sit down. Every time he sat down, he instantly stood up and didn't know what to do with himself.

The detective reviewed his notes. "Uh, huh. Okay, and what time did she leave for the Greenberg's?"

Before heading into the rain, Wayne yelled, "Glenda, we're gonna look around. Are you staying here?"

Although he couldn't see his wife, Laidlaw heard, "Yes, dear - I'm staying with the kids. Maker certain you dress warmly."

Rain pounded the trio as they left the house and Greg said, "Local teenagers hang out at the quarry and Riverbank Bridge. I'll check out the quarry, how about you two taking the bridge and look around Adventure Lake? Make sure you look thoroughly under the bridge."

Larry agreed entering his yard. "Sounds good, but we should get some decent clothes on. Wayne, I'll get my pickup and meet you out front ... all right?"

Running to his house, Wayne said, "Okay, just give me a couple of minutes."

Twenty minutes later, Greg thought a duck wouldn't be out in this weather, never mind two teenagers. Continually wiping water from his face, the detective had not seen a thing while watching wind-whipped sheets of rain crossing the beam of his powerful light methodically illuminating the terrain around the parking area of the old quarry. Thirty minutes of searching finally brought him back to the warmth of his station wagon, were he murmured, "Wherever they are, they're sure as hell not here."

Larry and Wayne thought the same as the wind and pelting rain hammered their vehicle manoeuvring the greasy dirt roads. The two men knew they were wasting their time. They had checked out the Riverbank Bridge area for more than an hour and spent an additional hour at Adventure Lake without seeing people, or another car.

Sandra Potts could not smell the peculiarly pungent odour of damp earth forming the walls, ceiling and floor of the natural soundproofed, unlit, six-by-eight-by-six foot chamber. For that matter, if the drugged girl had been able to open her eyes, she wouldn't have seen anything or heard anything. The teenager was cold and she lay in an awkward position on a threadbare mattress set on a small steel bunk against an earthen wall. A blindfold covered her eyes, her feet were bound together at her ankles, and someone had handcuffed both her wrists to a steel pipe fixed into the walls above and behind the head of the cot. The girl's jacket, shoes, and socks had been removed, and a fresh needle-hole marked the centre of her left arm.

As Sandra remained unconscious and shivering, a small opening appeared in the ceiling. After lowering a ladder, a dark-cloaked figure wearing two unlaced muddy sneakers climbed halfway down. For the next ten seconds a flashlight beam explored Sandra's shivering squalid hands, hair, face, sweater, pants and feet. The light lit up Sandra's face again before the person climbed out and pulled up the ladder.

MANIAC

Chapter 4

Normally Greg Britton took quick showers, but the morning after the downpour, he relaxed in the tub, trying to fit together the pieces of Sandra's disappearance.

Like his other two friends, Larry Sumislouski and Wayne Laidlaw, the police lieutenant had not returned home until after four in the morning. Although he still felt tired, the bleak morning offered no sympathy when he got up before his alarm clock sounded and opened the front door to retrieve his morning paper. The sun had no luck forcing its way through the clouds this day, and while the bathtub filled, Greg read the paper's massive headline: *Girl Disappears in Rapist's Territory.*

Lying back and trying to discern the rapist's moves in the area seemed impossible. Greg didn't have enough information, and before Sandra's disappearance, he really didn't give a damn anyway. Greg had seen and heard it all before. The world would always be full of weirdoes, and if there was one loose in this neighbourhood, so what?

What if the rapist didn't take her? Greg thought, soaping a scrubbing-brush and scrubbing his back. What if her boyfriend Philip was secretly holding her? It's happened before and it'll happen again. Yeah why not? In the past, he had questioned many senselessly jealous boyfriends, lovers and husbands that killed or maimed their loved ones in fits of anger. Young and old alike did it in the few seconds of self-centredness it took to ruin their lives. Most people don't think about the future when they get so angry that they take another person's life, or maim someone else. Later, they hand themselves in and couldn't give a damn about the court sentence. Then there are those that fit into two other categories; not caring less and ready to do it again, or disguising their action and running away rather than being caught.

Earlier when his eyes had opened, Greg had called Jim and Helen, and the distressed couple told him they hadn't heard anything, or the police weren't saying a word.

It was after his bath while Greg sat reading his newspaper and drinking a coffee that his phone rang. His face lit up the second his ear felt the earpiece.

"I'm fine, Jeff."

"Dad, I just read about Sandy. Any news?"

"Not yet, son. I was up half the night searching with Wayne and Larry. I'm just reading about it now."

"Stupid question, but how are Sandy's folks taking it? Have you spoken with them this morning?"

"Yeah, thirty minutes ago. They're going through hell."

"She was a bit of a flirt, Dad. What about her oddball friends?"

Greg frowned spilling a drop of coffee on the kitchen table and wiping it off with his free hand. "It's more serious than that, Jeff. Every teenager has oddball friends - even you had them. She's missing, missing. There's no doubt in my mind she's either dead, or she's been taken for use as a sex slave."

A pause took place before Jeff said, "Shit."

"But we'll get him ... we'll get the bastard."

"Wish I was there. Give Jim and Helen my love, Dad. Take care."

"I will, Jeff. Make sure you also take care of yourself. Love ya and see ya soon."

Greg hung up his phone, which rang again a few seconds later.

"What did you forget?"

The chuckle coming from the earpiece wasn't Jeff's. Rather, it was Greg's boss, Captain Samuel Csontos, saying, "My breakfast, that's what I forgot. Greg, it's me, Sam."

Sam wasn't a boss - he was more like a close friend, and Greg felt guilty he hadn't called the chubby, red-faced headman of homicide and robbery before now. Hell, he hadn't even called Wally Gaudry, his young easy going ex partner who was tying the knot in six weeks.

"Sam? Thought you were Jeff. How's the, uh, department doing?"

"Waiting for you to return. Jesus, Greg, have you become a hermit?"

"Yeah, so you're gonna have a long wait. What's up?"

Sam's voice turned more authoritative. "How long have you known Sandra Potts?"

Greg sat up and his face took on a more inquisitive expression. "Since her birth. Why, have you found her?"

"Not yet, but we've got her boyfriend, Philip Bayer. Do you know him?"

"Not really ... I've met him. Get to it, Sam, what's he saying?"

"He says he got a flat tire last night and Sandra walked or ran two blocks home alone."

"Who questioned him?"

"Your partner, Wally. This kid, er, Philip, has got a real problem, Greg."

"Why?"

"We've just seized his car. Sandra's shoes were on the back seat."

Greg stood for some reason, and when he sat back down again, Mickey jumped up on his lap. "What? She wouldn't walk home in her bare ... Have you booked him?"

"What do you think? There's blood on her shoes and on his clothes ... sure we've booked him."

Unconsciously biting his lower lip and slightly shaking his head, Greg asked, "Sam, have you told Jim and Helen Potts?"

"Not yet. Listen, can you come in this morning?"

"Why?"

"I just want to talk to you about this case."

"When?"

"Soon as you can. How about now?"

Greg checked his watch. "I can't. I'm going to the cemetery. How about eleven?"

The captain's voice sounded relieved. "Good. To show you I'm not such a bad bastard, I'll even buy lunch."

"You'll buy me lunch? Make that one minute to eleven."

Both men laughed and for a quick moment, Greg missed his job. After hanging up the phone, he wondered why he shouldn't go back. After all, his whole life was being a cop - a good cop, with intelligent efficient people around him. He had heard about corruption in police departments in similar sized cities, but not in this force. A long time ago someone had set standards and those standards had become the rule. Hell, maybe he should go back. Yeah, going back would take his mind off Diane. No, it wouldn't, because he wouldn't be able to visit the cemetery as often.

Seconds later he shook the idea of going back out of his mind.

When Lieutenant Greg Britton opened the door to the busy squad room where he had worked for so many years, he paused thinking nothing had changed in six months. Some cops used two fingers to type - others used only one. Some spoke loud, others kept their voices low. Throughout, the usual suspects or complainants sat whispering, yelling, or yielding just as the members did interviewing or interrogating them. Sitting next to, or across from police officers, criminals and witnesses chewed gum, blew smoke rings, drank stale coffee, cleaned their fingernails and fidgeted while expressing indifferent world-weary looks. Others just looked frightened, not allowing their wet wide eyes to miss a thing.

Why should the room change? Greg thought. Yeah, why? It was always full of the parasitic fraternity, arrested after getting greedy and taking more than their usual piece of life's pie.

Above all, the squad room's continuous noise amazed Greg. It consisted of a particular undecipherable frenzied buzz emanating from all directions day and night, but more so during the day. Like all police officers, he knew he was always awash in it but never realized he was being pulled under. During the day, his ears blocked out all sounds except the ones in which he was involved. But did that mean he blocked out all the other sights and sounds? Did other police officers also block them out? No way. He knew every spoken word and the scene that was always there. Some nights, some horrible nights, in the quiet of his bedroom when he couldn't sleep, his overactive subconscious mind insisted on revealing the precise details of every gruesome conversation whispered in the squad room. His mind also exposed the horrid scenes he'd seen, including viewing numerous crime scene photographs. When he was a rookie, he had to turn away from some of the bloody sights, including looking at certain photographs. After awhile, though, viewing blood and guts became mundane just like typing reports. Death and tragedy meant nothing. Whatever feelings he had didn't exist any longer.

What a difference, Greg thought, holding on to a small smile and nodding to associates while comparing the present setting to the peace and serenity of the cemetery he had just visited.

The words, "Hey, I'm over here. Where ya goin'?" stopped Greg from pondering and his insincere grin changed into an earnest smile mirroring that of his ex partner, Wally Gaudry.

Although Gaudry remained on the telephone, he stood covering the mouthpiece while giving Greg the thumbs up. "Greg, you're supposed to say hello to your number one partner when you enter this joint."

Continuing towards Csontos' office, the lieutenant replied, "I was gonna get around to it. Getting nervous yet?"

"About what?"

"Your wedding of course. Listen, the Captain's buying lunch; wanna join us?"

Gaudry eagerly sat down. "Free lunch? You bet!"

"You haven't changed, have ya, Wally?"

"What do ya mean? You usually stung me with the lunch tabs, remember?"

Both grins expanded as Greg indicated he understood and gave a half wave watching his partner get back to his telephone conversation. He liked Wally. The kid was real.

Captain Csontos recognized the lieutenant's three quick knocks. "Britton, what are ya doin'? My door's always open for you – get in here."

Greg slowly opened the door to the extremely fat captain's office, and grinned at its five-foot-ten occupant still dressed in clothes too small for his frame but a giant smile that wasn't.

Standing and offering his hand, Csontos' said, "Never thought we'd see you back. Even Wally missed ya."

"And you didn't?" Greg said, shaking Sam's hand, closing the door, and sitting in one of two worn out chairs. "Who the hell says I'm back?"

The black haired and moustached captain lowered his large frame back into its chair. "We all missed ya. How's it going?"

"A little easier now, thanks. Why the meeting?"

Sam's fat fingers explored a personnel document on his desk. "Before we get to that, your six months of leave expires in a week. Er…"

"No, I'm not coming back."

Csontos appeared a little saddened. "Why not? Greg, you're slated for my job in two years. What are you gonna do, fish your life away?"

"I don't fish … you fish. I Golf, but I don't fish."

"Golf, fish, what's the hell's the difference? Listen, I know what you're going through. That's probably the reason I never got married. I don't wanna get married, either. I wouldn't mind dating a nice looking woman, but that's about it. C'mon, Greg, I…"

The door opened after a light knock and Wally Gaudry's head appeared. "Is this about the Bayer kid?"

Greg motioned to Sam. "I uh, told Wally you're buying lunch."

"Shit, Gaudry, don't you ever buy?" Sam asked, pushing down on his chair's arms so the piece of furniture wouldn't join him as he stood to take his coat off the coat-rack standing next to him in the corner.

"Never, right Wally?" Greg asked.

Frustration secured Gaudry's face. "Bull shit! I'm the only one around here that does buy. Listen, I'm not joinin' you people to acquire the bullshit, er, intellectual knowledge the two of you believe you offer. I'm in here strictly for the free meal."

"How old are you, Wally?"

"Twenty-nine."

Chuckling, Sam said, "Well at twenty-nine you shouldn't eat that much. C'mon, if I'm buying, let's go."

All three indicated it felt good being together again, and during the short walk to their favourite restaurant, Sandra Potts' case came up. They were still discussing it when their meals arrived.

"So something's not right," Sam said, eating ribs, sharing his rib sauce with the world, and sipping the beer he ordered. Wally and Greg knew when their boss ordered ribs, it wasn't long before the sauce covered everything on and around the table.

"But what if it's not her blood?" Greg asked.

Sam had already covered his face with sauce, but he hadn't yet launched the brownish-red substance. "We'll know today. Crime lab has his clothes and her shoes. If this kid's lying, he's the best damned liar I've seen."

Greg finished half a glass of beer and asked, "What's his story? How's he account for the blood on his pants?"

"He doesn't. For some reason, he thinks we're setting him up. Says he got a flat and she wouldn't wait. It took him fifteen minutes to fix it and he went playin' pool before going home."

Greg nodded. "And the shoes?"

"Says she was wearin' 'em."

"Well certainly she'd be wearing them. The girl isn't going to walk home in the rain in her bare feet, is she?"

Wally wiped the table after the first blob of rib sauce landed. "Greg, have you ever spoken with this kid?"

"Yeah. He seems like a typical high school student. Not too bright, but a nice boy. Why?"

"We did a rundown on him. Nothing."

"He's only seventeen, what did you expect? How do we know he had a flat?" Greg asked.

Sam was now in the mood to share his rib sauce with the universe. "Wet flat in his trunk, and he put on one of those temporary jobs that was nearly worn out."

A moment later, Greg saw it coming but couldn't get out of the way fast enough. The liquid missile appeared to travel in slow motion, brilliantly guided to its target. Wiping it from his tie, Britton said, "So if he's been set up, maybe we're looking for a student?"

Throwing the last gnawed rib on the pile and grabbing his napkin, Sam leaned over the table and in a low voice asked, "How about talkin' to the kid for us?"

"What?"

"Greg, Greg, Greg, you know the boy. Who better but you? You've also known Sandy all her life, and probably the other boys she's dated. You're a natural for this one. How about it?"

"I've met him three times and now I'm his…? Get with it, Sam. I don't work here anymore."

"It'll help us," Sam said, pressing a little and using a pleading tone. I know you want out, so consider this your last case. Do it for the department, eh?"

The eyes of both detectives remained in Greg's face as he strummed his glass before taking a small sip. After about fifteen seconds, he said, "Okay, but what do you think I'll find that you two don't already know?"

"Shit, I don't believe it," Gaudry said, gently throwing his coffee spoon on the table.

Greg didn't have to be told; he knew his captain was the perpetual gambler. "Sam, you bet Wally I'd accept, didn't ya, you rotten bastard?"

Wiping his red chubby fingers and equally coloured grinning wet lips, Sam didn't need to reply, but he did speak to Gaudry after he finished massaging his mouth with his napkin. "Wally, you owe me twenty bucks. Nah, just pay the bill."

"You and your bets. What if I had said no?" Greg asked.

"Then I'd owe *him* twenty," Csontos confidently replied, pointing to Wally.

On the way out when Sam passed the bill to Wally, the youngest of three said, "Hey, I'd feel left out if I didn't get the opportunity to buy."

"And then I asked her if we could park behind her house for fifteen minutes. Like, uh … we were gonna neck."

What did she say?" Greg asked, taking notes in addition to taping his conversation with Philip Bayer. The boy looked different dressed in jail coveralls. Whenever he had seen Philip before, the tall muscular Elvis clone usually wore black denims rolled up a bit at the bottom, an unbuttoned white silk shirt, white socks and black penny-loafers.

The lieutenant and the Bayer boy had shared an interrogation room for over an hour since lunch, and Greg felt bloated.

Philip didn't like the line of questioning and it showed. Embarrassed, he said, "She said okay. I talked her into it. You don't think I'd hurt her do you?"

The police officer gazed coldly into the boy's eyes. "I dunno, would you? Have you ever had sexual intercourse with her?"

Adamantly, Philip replied, "No."

"Have you tried to get her in that mood?"

"You bet, er ... yeah, but Sandy always refused. She's ... still a virgin."

"How do you know that?"

"She told me."

"What about you?"

Greg leaned closer after an offensive look appeared on the boy's face, indicating he wasn't going to answer.

"I'm waiting. Look, Philip, you don't have to know why I'm asking these questions, and I can assure you your answers won't leave this building. Have you ever had a woman? Yes or no?"

Philip's voice became a whisper. "No, sir."

Greg sat back examining the boy's face. Guilt wasn't present, and all his years of police work told him Philip knew nothing about Sandra's disappearance.

"Well, my boy, someone who doesn't like you placed Sandra's shoes on the back seat of your car. Do you always leave your car parked in front of your house?"

"Yes, sir."

"Unlocked?"

"Not usually. That night I was soaked, so I just ran into the house and forgot about locking the car."

"Phil, where do you and Sandra normally go necking?"

"The lake ... or sometimes the quarry."

"That's what I thought. And that's where you took her last night?"

Philip shook his head. "No, sir … like I've told you I…"

"Got any enemies?" Greg asked, cutting him off.

"Not that I know of … at least no one that would do this to me. Do you think Sandy's all right, sir?"

Greg took a deep breath and let it out slowly. "I don't know, son, but I sure hope so. Now, I want you to think hard. Is there anything you can think of that you haven't told me or the other police officers?"

Philip had decided there wasn't before his eyes indicated there might be. "No … well, maybe."

The boy received Greg's full attention. "What?"

"At first the jack fell out. When I was pumpin' it up again, I stopped to see where she was. I saw her running around the corner."

"What corner, Philip?"

"Hemlock Street."

The lieutenant wrote the street name down, circled it, and asked, "You saw her run around the corner on Hemlock? Two blocks away?"

"You bet … er, yes, sir."

"You're certain about that?"

"Yes, sir. There's a streetlamp there. She was easy to see. Sandy was wearin' white jeans and shoes."

Greg pushed so hard his pencil broke. Sharpening it, he said, "Okay, let me get this straight. You get a flat on Collingswood, halfway between Walnut and Maple. She takes off home. She stays on Collingswood, crosses Maple, keeps going and turns left on Hemlock? Is that right? You definitely saw her turn left on Hemlock?"

"Yes, sir, and I wasn't worried because once she'd turned, she was only…"

The police officer offered a questioning look before he cut the boy off. "Half a block from the back of her house."

Philip swallowed and nodded. "Yes, sir. She was nearly home."

Thinking, Greg tapped the eraser end of the pencil on the table about ten times before asking, "Phil, how do you account for the blood on the driver's side of the front seat in your car, and the rear of your pants?"

"I cut my hand on the pop machine at the pool hall."

"But how would you get blood on her shoes?"

"No idea, sir. I never touched her shoes. She wouldn't walk home in her bare feet. It was really raining. I ... I don't know how her shoes got in my car."

"When did you drop out of school, Philip?"

"Two months ago, but I'm goin' back."

Greg indicated to the boy that continuing his education would be a good move. "Uh, why didn't you go home after you fixed the flat?"

"I've already told you."

"Tell me again."

"I was pissed off. I went back to the pool hall ... it's open all night."

"Pissed off at what?" Greg asked, already knowing the reason but wanting to hear it again.

"That she wouldn't wait and let me drive her home."

"Are you sure they read you your rights when they arrested you?"

"Yes, sir, and I'm not hiding anything."

Greg extended his hand, and said, "That concludes my questions for Philip Bayer." After turning off the tape recorder, he stood, and headed to the door. "You wait here, son."

"You mean ... I ... I can't go home?"

Hesitating at the door, Greg reluctantly said, "No, not yet. That blood has to be checked, and if it's Sandy's, get your parents to hire a lawyer. By the way ... you wouldn't be an Elvis fan in this day and age would you?"

"You can totally bet I am."

"Thought so."

At the same time as Greg walked towards Captain Csontos' office, a dark figure wearing the same dirty untied sneakers closed the hatch after partially climbing down a ladder he had just lowered into Sandra Potts' *tomb*.

Upon reaching the bottom, the man ripped the blindfold off the terrified girl's face and unleashed the full force of his flashlight's beam into her eyes, forcing Sandra to recoil violently from the pain. Even with the covering off her eyes, the sudden ache made it impossible for Sandra to see anything and she couldn't rub her eyes because her arms remained handcuffed to the pipe.

The figure finally turned off his flashlight and switched on a tiny bulb dangling from an electrical cord hanging from a hook screwed into the dirt ceiling. As Sandra's eyes slowly became accustomed to the low light, she discovered her dingy confines and the eerie heavy breathing stationary figure standing near her. The combination made the teenage girl realize the hopelessness of her plight and she began struggling, emitting vocal sounds from her nose and taped mouth.

Quickly taking off his gloves, the man used one hand to rip the adhesive tape from his prisoner's mouth while his other hand cupped her lips so hard she could barely breathe let alone scream. When he eased the pressure, he used a finger to trace an ear-to-ear line across the girl's throat. Sandra instantly recognized her captor's warning and stopped struggling.

The two stared at each other for a good thirty seconds before the hooded man placed his right forefinger vertically across his mouth and swivelled his head from side to side indicating there would be problems if she screamed or fought him.

Sandra didn't know what to do, try or think. Since being kidnapped, her mind had roamed constantly, opening a hundred scenarios, some gruesome, some even with her father dressed in golden armour riding a white mount and coming to her rescue. But this was not another dream, and when the man took a pair of scissors from a pocket and held them up showing them to her, the girl's heart skipped and she screamed yelling, "Someone please help me! Oh, please help me!"

The man knew no one could hear the girl, but that didn't matter, she had disobeyed him. After forming a fist with his right hand, he hit her face so hard the blow fractured her left cheekbone, loosened two of her teeth, and knocked her out. When she came to, moaning, her captor was in the process of cutting the front of her sleeveless sweater from the hem to the neck. Sandra struggled as hard as she could and tried to shift her body away, but the scissors continued cutting through the sweater's top.

Finally, when he finished, the man ripped the garment off her, threw it to the floor, and stood back beholding the beauty of his prize, now only wearing a brassiere on her heaving upper body.

Sandra knew her captor wasn't about to leave the job *unfinished*, but she had no control over her body. She couldn't stop shaking as she moved frantically to stop the crazed groaning maniac from unzipping her pants and ripping them down with her panties. When he got them off her, he threw the items on the floor before ripping off her brassiere and standing back again observing the Goddess he had waited so long to seduce. A Goddess so terribly frightened she didn't know her name. Sandra could hardly breathe or speak, her filthy hair covered her sticky face and although her skin felt cold and damp, steam rose off her throbbing stomach and heaving breasts.

Delirious and totally worn out, Sandra couldn't see or feel the cuts the handcuffs had made to her wrists, or the new blood running down her arms after mixing with dried blood. She didn't really know if this was a dream or if it was hell and she was having her own personal meeting with the devil. Now oblivious to any form of civilized reality, the girl couldn't understand why this whimpering man wearing a hood and standing over her had allowed his pants and shorts to fall to the floor. The youngster's mind just wouldn't allow her to reason any longer. She couldn't do anything to stop his strong hands grabbing the inside of her thighs, to force her legs open.

MANIAC

Chapter 5

On his way back to Captain Csontos' office, Greg Britton considered all aspects of his discussion with Philip Bayer. Even before knocking on the Captain's door, the lieutenant had concluded the boy was innocent.

As far as Greg was concerned someone other than Philip had taken the girl, and it probably was the local rapist. Jealous sweethearts didn't do this, and besides, Sandy hadn't really been serious about boys until Philip came along. Oh sure, his son Jeff said she was a bit of a flirt, but that was Sandra's way. She'd smile, wink, and then back of quickly. The girl also obeyed her mother and father's rules about being in on time, and she listened to her mother about not having sex so young.

"Can we put him back in the cells?" Sam asked, motioning Greg to sit down.

"Yeah, I'm through with him."

Csontos picked up his telephone and after pressing three buttons and saying, "Lock up the Bayer boy," he returned his attention to Greg. "Well, what do you think?"

Britton shrugged, saying, "The same as you. He's been set up."

Sam Csontos scratched his huge belly, breathed in deeply, raised his glass to the ceiling, and slowly released the air. When his eyes focused on Greg again, he picked a paper up from his desk and handed it to the lieutenant.

About five seconds after he put his glasses on, Greg's forehead creased. "Jesus … Sandra's blood?"

Sam nodded. "On her shoes, the seat of his car, and on his pants. I've phoned his parents … they're coming over with a lawyer."

"How do you know it's her blood type?"

"Wally checked her medical records. It sure as hell isn't his blood. He's ordered a DNA test."

Reading the paper again, Greg said, "It doesn't make any sense. Why would he keep her shoes?"

"Nothing makes sense about this case. What did he tell you?" Sam said, opening a drawer on his desk and uncapping a bottle of indigestion tablets. Before taking two, he added, "Did you learn anything new?"

Greg handed the report back. "The same as he told Wally, except he saw her turn left on Hemlock Street."

Sam's curious reaction imitated Greg's earlier response with Philip. "That places her…"

Both men nodded when Greg said, "Yep, just about at the back of her house. A half block away."

While Britton placed his glasses in their case, Wally Gaudry knocked and his head appeared. "Got a sec?"

"Yeah, what is it?" Sam asked.

Wally passed a typewritten sheet to the captain, and said to Greg, "A black and white found Sandra's jacket at the quarry, and papers from her homework at the lake."

The statement amazed both police officers.

Wally continued, "There's blood on both, and I rushed the tests. Guess what?"

"Surprise me," Greg replied. "What next?"

Sam rubbed his eyes passing the paper to Greg. "Christ, read this."

"Let me save you the time," Gaudry said. "Philip's blood is on her jacket, but it's hers on her homework."

Sam's face firmed and when his large body briskly stood nearly taking the chair with him, he took the paper from Greg's hands. "Wally, charge the kid."

"Are you sure?" Britton asked, also standing.

As if directing traffic, Csontos held his right hand up in front of the lieutenant. "I know the difference between rain and being pissed on, Greg, so do you. Wally, you heard me … charge the bastard and read him his rights *again*."

That afternoon, Greg Britton didn't enter his house after parking his car. On his way home, he decided to visit Jim and Helen to see how they were managing.

It wasn't a pretty scene when he entered and said hello to Wayne and Glenda Laidlaw, and Larry and Joan Sumislouski, also visiting. Greg had never seen Jim Potts look so bad. The man's eyes appeared red raw and he needed a shower and a shave.

Britton knew the house always looked lived in. It was never neat and the furniture was a little worn, but it was cosy and clean. This time dishes filled the sink and countertop and every room appeared neglected.

"Where's Helen," Greg asked, sitting down in the living room with his five friends.

"Jim took her to the hospital earlier in the day," Larry said, caringly. "Only he can visit her. Helen's nerves are totally shot and the doctors are quite worried."

Greg nodded. "So they should be with what she's going through. What about Merriam and Christine?"

"They're with Helen's sister," Joan replied.

"There's a rumour on the radio that Philip's been charged. Has he?" Wayne asked.

Greg never liked discussing cases with friends whether he was involved or not, and it showed. "Yeah, he's been charged," he said, before changing the subject. "Jim, we know what you're going through, old buddy, but hang in there."

Sandra's dad didn't acknowledge the police officer's compassion. Instead, he stood and walked to the fireplace. Placing his head on his hands that were grabbing the mantelpiece, Jim quietly sobbed.

All five neighbours felt Jim's anguish. Greg stood next to him and placed his right arm around his friend's shoulders. "I said, we all know what you're going through, Jim. Many people are working on this case and thing's will work out all right." Turning his head towards Joan Sumislouski, he asked, "Who's looking after your boys?"

"Madge came over and offered," Joan said, adding, "You know, I think she's a nice person, and I never knew she attends church every Sunday."

"She might be religious but she can curse," Greg said. "I've heard her telling Jehovah's Witnesses to 'Get the hell off my porch.' She doesn't hold back on profanity."

"If there was only something we could do," Larry said, his face sharing Jim's defeated look. "Christ, I feel helpless as hell. If this happened to us, life wouldn't be worth living. Jim, dear friend, try to be positive; I'm sure she'll be all right."

Glenda motioned to Greg. "Joan's going to give me a hand tidying up the house and we're going to do their laundry."

"That nice of you," Greg said, compassionately. "They need all the help they can get. Jim, Jim…"

Jim Potts slowly raised his head. "What?" he whispered.

"Try and pull yourself together. Right now, Helen, Merriam and Christine need all the strength and comfort you can give them."

A lost appreciative smile appeared before Jim placed his head back in his hands. "I'd like to kill that son-of-a-bitch."

Glenda moved next to Jim and gently rubbed his back. "Jim, dear, you have a nice shower while we're cleaning the house, and then we'll drive you to visit Helen."

The three men had helped the girls clean the Potts' house, and just before Wayne and Glenda drove Jim to the hospital, the lieutenant found himself accepting Larry and Joan's invitation to supper, with, of all people, Madge Grant.

The aroma of Shepherd's Pie with a selection of garden vegetables filled the Sumislouski house when the three arrived at dinner. The two boys didn't sit at the same table because Joan had rented their favourite video and cooked hotdogs for them, which they ate in the den.

"Someone was in my bedroom closet two nights ago," Madge said, picking away at her vegetables. "Probably came in while I spoke with the police officer."

Although totally unintentional and unseen by Madge, the smile creeping over Greg's lips moved to Larry and Joan Sumislouski's faces, when the lieutenant said, "Are you sure it was your bedroom closet ... not your hall closet? Madge, are you hallucinating about that young WWF wrestler falling in love with you again?"

Britton had never seen Madge really smile, but he realized he enjoyed seeing her blush, saying, "Oh, Heaven's no, not him. I'm over him. No, this *visitor* wore muddy footwear ... they soiled my white shoes in the closet, and my carpet."

"Are you sure it wasn't my cat?" Greg found himself asking. "According to what I hear, Mickey spends more time in your house than mine."

Madge grinned again and her face maintained its reddish tone. "It might have been if Mickey's taken to wearing size ten-and-a-half sneakers."

With the joking over with, Greg turned serious, asking, "What time was this? And why did you call the police?"

"What? Don't lower your voice. Speak up, Sonny!"

Just the way Madge had mentioned the word, "sneakers," got Greg grinning again. "I asked, what time did it happen? And why did you call the police?"

"I'm not too sure, but it was after midnight. I saw a man in that exact same spot the previous night as well. I also gave that information to the police. They're lookin' in my closet right now."

Greg knew about the first sighting because Larry had mentioned it at the golf course. He made a mental note to speak to Wally about the current sighting.

"Hah, so it was you?" Larry said, aiming his eyes at Madge but transferring them to his wife. "Joan, there's our culprit. A cop pounded on our door after midnight and woke everyone up."

"What did he want?" Greg asked.

Just after Joan said, "Someone reported a man jumping over our fence," Larry said, "Joan stayed with the kids, and I searched our lot, the alley, and the neighbourhood for half-an-hour without any luck. There was a cop out front doing the same, and I joined the one checking out the back. I would have told Jim but I thought he might be sleeping. Jesus, Madge, if you're going to start seeing people jump over fences, how about doing it during the day. The person you saw on Friday night was Jim putting his garbage cans out."

Looking smug and shaking her head, Madge said, "Oh no, it wasn't. I can tell the difference between Jim Potts at night and Jim Potts during the day. Jim had already put his garbage cans out. I've seen two people at Sandra's window."

"Two people?" Greg and Larry asked simultaneously.

"Yes, two people, but not at the same time. On Friday, the person disappeared while I got my binoculars, but early Sunday the son-of-a ... er, the man jumped over your fence. That's the goddamned ... uh, that's the truth. I think they've been at that window a few times because I've seen men skulking up and down the lane at night."

Madge's unshakeable opinion deposited worried looks on Larry and Joan. It also placed a questioning expression on Greg's face. Now, more than ever, he wanted to get involved.

When Larry asked why she thought two people were involved, Madge said she didn't want to discuss it anymore. "The police have all my statements."

Greg had enjoyed the evening at Larry and Joan's, and later while watching television at home, images of old Madge Grant kept going through his mind. Seeing his elderly neighbour from across the alley in person rather than knowing she was hiding behind her drapes was completely different. He knew she wasn't the old bitch he kept making her out to be. Madge had raised four kids, held a good job as an ambulance dispatcher and had the guts to look after herself and live alone. Even following her husband's death, Madge put her eldest son through university. Greg knew she had received a hefty sum from Horace's life insurance policy, and he knew she shared it with her kids and never quit work. It was in Madge's blood to pitch in and make her country great, and as a proud member of the Daughters of the American Revolution, she did just that. As far as her statement about two people creeping around Sandy's window, Greg thought Madge was wrong. It was probably the same man but crouching a little lower.

Did Sandra know there were peeping toms at her window? Probably not, he thought. Then again, why did she leave her curtains open so people could look inside? Did she like teasing people? No, Sandra was just an innocent teenager with a wonderful personality and a beautiful body, Greg concluded.

Mickey jumped up on Greg's lap while the officer started reassessing his views of Madge Grant, and Sandy. After all these years, he was close to actually liking Madge. The old bird wasn't too bad after all. "I guess anyone would get upset if a cat kept coming in to piss everywhere," he mumbled to

Mickey. "But how did you get into this habit of visiting Madge?"

Just as Greg was going to ask his cat another question, a disclosure the television news announcer mentioned, caught the lieutenant's attention.

"...and at this time police are not releasing full details concerning the missing girl. It is known charges have been laid against Sandra's seventeen-year-old boyfriend, but police public relations officer Sergeant Haissam Jundi has not revealed the nature of the charges. In other news..."

Gently moving Mickey to one side, the detective got up and picked up a photo of Jeff from the mantelpiece. His son looked so young and innocent like Philip. Yeah, just like Philip, he kept thinking. Like Philip, like Philip, like Philip. "Philip isn't guilty," he murmured. "If anything, he loved Sandra. So some son-of-a-bitch is setting him up and that son-of-a-bitch has Sandra or has killed her."

When Greg sat down after returning the picture, he knew he had to make the decision he had kept putting off. Did he want to leave the force or not? Probably, but he wasn't certain. Would Diane have wanted him to quit? No, except for the night shift she was his biggest supporter all those years he wanted out. She would want him to stay. She always asked him what he would do with himself if he resigned.

"Well, I'm not gonna take up painting, that's for sure," he said, stroking his stubble and searching for a small book in his back right pocket. Flipping pages while wandering into the kitchen, the lieutenant picked up the telephone, punched out a number and sat back.

"Hi Elsie," he said to Sam's sister. "It's Greg Britton. Good, how are you? Great ... Yeah, those were the days. Er, is he in? Sure, thanks..."

Greg heard the phone being placed down, picked up again, and a voice saying, "Is this the obstinate lieutenant?"

"Hi Sam. Can we make a deal?"

"Depends on what kind of a deal?"

"Extend my leave for a month and give me the Potts' case."

Sam whistled. "You've brightened my day, but there's a problem."

"Oh?"

"Ya didn't give enough notice so I can't pay ya for the month. That is unless you're permanently coming back?"

"I'm not certain yet."

"Uh, would you mind calling it *voluntary* duty?"

A small pause and a grin preceded, "Thanks, Sam … see you tomorrow."

Greg was about to hang up, but his boss said, "Hey, you're not such a stubborn bastard after all."

"Yeah I am. See ya at eight."

"Here, I saved it for you," Sam Csontos said, handing Greg a holstered semi-automatic pistol.

Britton accepted the weapon and placed it on the captain's desk. "Thanks, what would I do without you?"

Greg hadn't slept much the night before, and when he arrived at work early dressed in a crisp business suit, his fellow employees going off shift hadn't recognized him. Even Wally had kept a straight face saying, "The District Attorney's office isn't in this building - it's down the block."

"You need me just as much as I need you, Greg Britton, and don't you forget it," Csontos mouthed, eating the balance of a sandwich and hitting a waste paper basket eight feet away with the crumpled waxed paper.

"Yeah I probably do. But you know damned well. Philip Bayer's not guilty, and some of my close friends are going out of their minds."

Sam took out his wallet and counted his bills. "Fifty bucks says the kid did it."

"You're on," Greg said. Who's workin' on this with Wally?"

"Allan Dabbit and Mel Holmes. Do you know them?"

Thinking for a moment, Greg nodded. "Yeah, I saw 'em at the Potts' house, and other rape cases before they passed their detective exams."

"Yeah, same guys," Sam said, popping two indigestion tablets. "Want some?" he asked offering the jar.

"Thanks anyway. I don't think you should be taking them, Sam. I hear they can really screw up a person's sex life. Uh, let's keep my involvement out of the press and on the quiet. Okay?"

Before putting the pills away, the captain tried to read the small print on the bottle. "Are you sure?"

"Sure I'm sure. I've told my son and friends I wouldn't be back."

"No, no, Greg. I mean, are you sure these are not good for my sex life?"

Grinning, Greg asked, "Would I shit ya?"

"Probably. Why would you stop at this late stage of your life? Anyway, another fifty says you'll change your mind and stay on the force."

"Then I've made a hundred today," Britton said, looking cocky.

"Hey, do I look like a sucker?" the captain asked, making note of the bets and placing the piece of paper in his shirt pocket. "Money's my sixth sense."

Greg picked up his weapon, and after standing, said, "I hope it works better than the other five."

Csontos' immense belly rolled when he laughed. "Welcome back, Greg. Now, take this file and get the hell outta here."

Greg retained a steady grin as he strolled the short distance to Wally Gaudry's desk. His partner had just hung up his phone. "What's so funny?"

"Csontos' gut always makes me laugh. I have Sandra's file - you grab the other rape files, and your coats. Where are Dabbit and Holmes?"

Gaudry piled some folders together. "Over at the Bayer house. Hey, can't I even welcome you back?"

"What was that?" Greg asked, trying not to laugh.

"I said, can't I even welcome you back?"

Greg began walking away. "That's what I thought you said. Sure you can welcome me back officially, rather than mentioning I work for the district attorney. You can buy lunch."

"Shit I knew it," Gaudry grunted, putting on his Harris Tweed jacket and London Fog raincoat before picking up the files. "Where're we going?"

"The quarry."

On the way to quarry it became increasingly obvious that Wally had missed working with Greg because the young detective never stopped talking as he drove his partner down country roads with little traffic. During the trip, Gaudry briefed Britton on personnel changes, modifications to regulations, and what was happening on the rape cases. The usual suspects had been pulled in and released. Released prisoners with previous sexual problems or those on parole had also been questioned, but nothing had been learned.

"We've got a cunning new creep doing these things, Greg, and he's going be tough to catch. Oh, and just so you know, three of us have checked out the Goslings ... there's nothing going on there."

"Did you go in their house?"

"No, but ..."

"Then how do you know they're not involved?"

"Well, let's just say I don't believe they're involved. I spoke with old man Gosling and he says he hasn't been letting Ronnie out."

The lieutenant's ears remained perked while listening to his partner, but nothing stood out. Greg wanted to hear that great revelation that formed the basis of solving all cases, but it wasn't there.

What if Madge was right? Greg thought. What if there were two involved? "Wally, who checked out the pool hall?"

"I did, and the info is on the file. The kid was there from just after nine-thirty to somewhere around midnight. He came back around twelve-forty-five and played until one-thirty."

"Do his parents know what time he got home?"

"No, but a hospital worker from across the street did. She pulled into her driveway as Philip arrived home. She said he got home at two on the button, and ... she's known him since he was a kid."

Greg sighed. "He still is a kid ... and talk about being organized, he fixes a flat, travels to the lake, the quarry, and the pool hall, and is home by two. Shit, Superman couldn't do better than that."

Rain started splattering the windshield and Wally turned on the wipers. "Mel Holmes has discovered the quarry is next to an old mine shaft that closed in the fifties."

The lieutenant already knew. "Yeah, they were going to build a complex to house the state government if the balloon went up. I thought they flooded it?"

"Not yet. Dabbit is getting maps. There are a lot of old tunnels and caves down there."

"Who found her jacket?"

"Unit twenty on patrol," Wally said, turning off the paved road and proceeding along a parallel gravel road.

"Was it hidden?"

"No. In a few minutes I'll show you where it was found."

When their car entered a clearing, Wally pulled over in what appeared to be a well-travelled area and both police officers got out. The clearing was a natural space in the middle of tall hills, and other than the now hammering rain the area was silent.

"This is where her windbreaker was found," Gaudry said, pointing to a small bush.

Whistling, Greg walked around the car to where Wally stood, took a deep breath and gave his partner an offended look.

"What?" Gaudry asked, recognizing Britton's scoffing at the simplicity of the find.

"Wally, I've been here before, and it wasn't lying around then."

"But that was at night, Greg. It was dark and perhaps you couldn't…?"

Gaudry followed Britton sauntering over to a stand of small trees. When Greg stopped, he said, "I parked where we just did and I covered every inch of this entrance area. I also left my headlights on and carried a Big-Bertha light. Sure it was pissing rain like it is now but I'd see a blue windbreaker – the lining is white for Christ's sake."

Wally glanced around. "Yeah, you probably would."

"Has the pit been searched?" Britton asked, looking perturbed at the mud now covering his shoes.

Gaudry nodded. "And the surrounding bush." Glancing at Greg's shoes, he said, "And don't look at me … I ain't cleaning or shining 'em."

Both officers snickered and Greg placed his left arm around his partner's shoulders. "Let's go look at the mine."

Wally nearly got the car stuck driving out of the quarry's parking area, and five minutes later with their car's windshield wipers going full out, the vehicle pulled around on the only dirt road heading towards the mine's entrance. It didn't take long to reach the other side of the large crater, and a locked chain fence crossing the road.

"Got a tire wrench?" Greg asked, getting out.

"Yeah, I think so."

After breaking the barrier, Greg mouthed, "No more lock."

Re-entering the car, Wally said, "You just broke the fence, and the law."

"Whatever," Britton replied, more concerned with his shoes than the lock.

The senior of the two didn't think they accomplished too much that afternoon. The main entrance to the mineshaft was closed, and later when both detectives got out of their car at the police garage, dried mud covered their shoes and lower pant legs.

"I'm taking these files home," Greg said, patting the paperwork that should have remained in the building.

Walking towards the elevator door, Gaudry replied, "I know nothing."

A sly smile occupied the lieutenant's face. "That's what I like to hear. Listen when you're in the office, ask Dabbit if he's picked up the maps. Call me later."

Just as Gaudry pushed the up button, Greg yelled, "Hey, Wally!"

The empty elevator's door opened. "What?"

"Thanks for lunch. Are you buying again tomorrow?"

"Probably, Goddamnit," Gaudry yelled.

Greg nodded appreciatively. "Great, I haven't eaten steak since the barbecue."

Waving as he entered the elevator, Wally slyly grinned muttering, "That's nice, because you won't be gettin' any tomorrow, either."

Earlier, the lieutenant had managed to park his car in a covered lot only two blocks from the police garage; when he pulled up behind Larry Sumislouski's garage his clothes were still damp from the walk.

"Hi Larry - Day off?" he said, watching his friend working on the old Ford, and a stranger doing some wiring on the back porch.

Larry appeared a little tired, coming over to Greg's car. "Nah, but I only put in a half-day. This thing is getting to Joan and me, Greg. Both of us offered a small prayer for Sandra last night, and then we couldn't sleep after what Madge said. There have been two detectives in Jim and Helen's place all day, and I just got back from driving Jim to the hospital."

Greg turned off his windshield wipers. "This weather doesn't help my state of mind either."

"They say mental stress is worse than physical stress. Working on this car helps take my mind off the situation,"

Larry said, using a small tool to tighten Greg's outside mirror. "Joan is so tense she wants to move away from this neighbourhood and even at age six the boys are nervous about going out. I've just signed a petition someone brought around asking city hall to put more police cars in our area. They've left a petition paper on your back porch."

Greg shook his head. "Forget it, there's three here already; we won't get any more. Who's the guy on your porch?"

"He's installing our new burglar alarm."

"How's Jim taking it?"

Sauntering back to the Ford, Larry said, "Don't ask. He's sick to his stomach and Customs have given him three weeks off. Anything new?"

"Not that I know of. How's Helen?"

"Still in hospital but Jim says she's settling down a bit. She can have visitors now, and after I got back, Joan took the boys to see her. I'll be going tonight with Wayne and Glenda. Wanna come?"

Greg had driven a few feet, but he stopped again. "Can't tonight, Larry. What part are you working on today?"

"Replacing the old starter. How the hell do they come out?"

"If I can recall, you would be better off undoing the bottom bolt first," Greg replied.

"Thank God I started this project. I'd probably be the same as Jim if I didn't have something to do at home," Larry said, his face appearing forlorn. Find Sandra, Greg. Jim and Helen can't take much more of this."

"I know, Buddy … and we will. Pass along my love and tell them I'll see them soon."

After parking his car, Greg used his free arm to carry his wet cat up the back stairs. He used an old towel hung on a hook to dry Mickey off, and the cat jumped down before the lieutenant dumped the files on the kitchen table, shut the door and turned on the lights.

After throwing his damp overcoat over the back of a chair, Greg noticed the blinking light indicating two calls on his answering machine. They turned out to be a call from Mel Holmes, and one from Jeff.

"Hi, Dad, it's me. When you get a chance, give me a call. Thanks."

"Greg, it's Mel. I thought you might have come up to the office after you visited the mine. Found Sandra's diary today and there's some interesting stuff. If you can, please give me a call, soonest."

Mickey jumped on Greg's lap and quickly got put back down before the curious lieutenant wiped off his pant legs, exchanged dirty looks with the cat now washing itself and took his small address book out of his back pocket. A few moments after looking up Mel Holmes' number, he had Mel on the phone. "What's up?"

"We found Sandra's diary between her mattress and the box spring. Philip's been diddling her a bit, but..."

"Any intercourse?"

"No, but he's got roving hands. I guess we all did at that age."

"What do you mean at that age?" Greg asked, not realizing a wet cat had jumped back on his knee. "Christ, I don't know about you, but I'm not dead yet. When it comes to the fairer sex, we're supposed to have roving hands."

Holmes cleared his throat. "Uh, yeah I guess so. Er, someone in your neighbourhood's been following her. No, let me rephrase that. She doesn't say she was being followed, she says he's showing up at the oddest places, like the grocery store across from her school, and other spots."

"What other places?" Greg asked, not noticing that Mickey was now on his left knee again.

"Outside the local swimming pool, or two or three rows behind her in the movies, or passing or walking behind her in the mall."

"Why do you say this guy's from our neighbourhood?"

"Because she says she doesn't want to get her mom and dad involved. Doesn't want to create problems in the hood."

Greg rolled his eyes to the ceiling and lightly shook his head. "In the *hood?* Mel, you're seeing too many teenage movies. Any calls from the public?"

"Give me a break, Lieutenant," Holmes retorted in a full-throated voice. "*Hood* isn't my word, it's hers. She says she wants to keep peace in the *hood*. No, not a single call."

"Anything else?"

"Yeah, she said she's afraid of him, and she might tell you."

Mel Holmes' words echoed loudly through Greg's mind. "She wrote that she might tell me? Is that what you said?"

"Yeah."

"Where's the diary now?"

"At the office."

"Good, I'd like to see it tomorrow. Anything else?"

"Yeah, just one other thing. On a page by itself, she says Brentsen is one major head case, and he scares her."

When Greg stood, Mickey fell off his knee and began nonchalantly washing his paws before giving his house friend another bad-tempered look.

"Forget it, Mickey. I'm not getting this suit cleaned again because of you."

"What was that? Holmes asked.

Greg returned his attention to the phone. "I'm talking to my cat. Check with Sandra's chums at school and see if they know this Brentsen. I'll be in early tomorrow. Just a minute, did you ask Sandra's parents if they know someone by that name?"

"That's the first thing I did, and drew a blank."

"Okay, Mel, thanks ... keep me posted."

Greg didn't rise for any particular reason, so when he sat down again, and hung up the telephone, he got another shot of the evil eye from Mickey.

"Not one call," Greg murmured to himself as he punched out Jeff's number. The police had placed numerous photographs of Sandra in the local newspapers, issued handbills showing her photograph, and television announcements still rolled with her picture, but no one had called.

"What's this bastard's game?" he mumbled. "Has he killed her, or...? Hi, Jeff."

"Thanks for calling, Pop. The exam I took today covered the McLennan case."

"McLennan case? Never heard of it, Charlie Brown."

"We've had quite a few rape and murder cases in this area, Dad, but one always stands out. Surely you remember the rapes taking place at Everton, Cooksville and Breckville and they charged a guy by the name of Anthony McLennan but he got off."

"Oh, yeah, now I remember. About seven years ago ... his DNA saved his ass."

Right, they got the wrong guy, Dad. The rapes and the murders of young girls remain unsolved. The police were sure McLennan was linked, but they never got him. He's a minister today."

"What are you getting at, Jeff?"

"Dad, clear your head. Everything is similar. The Everton rapist always attacked blond girls under eighteen, and he always struck around midnight and took their panties with him."

Greg began doodling on top of a file folder. "Are you sure?"

After chuckling, Jeff asked, "Hey, am I ever wrong?"

"That's my line, Kiddo."

"Sorry, Dad, can I have it?"

"It's yours. Thanks, Jeff, I'll check up on the McLennan case. When are you coming home?"

"Shortly ... I'll call you."

"Okay, Son. God Bless. I love you."

"You too, Dad."

After placing the telephone down, Greg sat back for a moment. Yeah, he had forgotten about the McLennan case, or as the press called it, *The Panty Box Rapist.* A box of soiled girls' panties left on the steps of the police station had the whole department working overtime. Finally, when the police tracked down the owners, every girl had been a victim, and some had not reported their ordeal. The rapes stopped at about the time the box was left, and the police couldn't understand why the marauder hadn't burned the garments. Instead, he had left them to be found.

"Because he enjoyed taunting the police, and he killed a girl before leaving the place," Greg muttered, getting up and feeding Mickey. "Or maybe I should say he enjoys taunting us. It's the same fiend. The bastard is so goddamned sure of himself. Yeah, I forgot about the Everton case. Jeff, you're a chip off the old block."

MANIAC

Chapter 6

Although tired, Greg Britton didn't go to bed after speaking with his son Jeff, and Detective Mel Holmes. The police lieutenant had much catching up to do and his routine changed that night. Before taking off his jacket and loosening his tie, Greg placed his semi-automatic in a high cupboard and then searched around gathering four coloured pencils. After giving Mickey a saucer of milk and some dry cat food, he opened the first file and began reading.

Later that evening, two empty coffee cups sat next to a full glass of milk in front of the lieutenant as he continued studying the printed material. He had even brought in the reading lamp from the front room, and when he checked his watch at midnight, open files covered the table, and three empty beer bottles stood next to the other containers. His wife had bought those beers, and nine other identical bottles remained in the fridge.

At two-thirty in the morning, Greg took off his glasses, rubbed his eyes, closed the last file, moved Mickey off his lap and before stacking the files and his notes, cleared off the table.

"Interesting," he said, walking towards his bedroom after checking the front and back doors and turning off the lights.

While Greg Britton snored gently, a hooded figure left a small bulb burning in Sandra Potts' bemired chamber, climbed the ladder and bolted the hatch behind him.

This was the man's second trip out of the tomb. After cutting off her clothing, he had removed one pair of handcuffs, leaving the other pair holding Sandra's swollen right wrist to the pipe. He had also taken away the girl's body-waste bucket, emptied it and brought it back. The trembling teenager sitting on the bunk and covered only by a blanket had prayed he wouldn't return, but before his unlaced sneakers touched the last rung, he threw a thermos next to her and a wrapped sandwich at her to catch. Sandra didn't attempt to grasp the food, so the waxed paper pouch hit her head and fell to the ground.

Sandra Potts couldn't look at the man picking up the sandwich and throwing it again at her swollen face. Sobbing and keeping her face fixed at the mud floor, she drew up her legs and cupped them with her left hand. This action didn't please her abductor and he grabbed her ankles, pulled them down stretching her body out before snatching the blanket and throwing it aside.

Sandra didn't feel the pain of her festering right wrist, and her uncontrollable sobbing became louder as the man pushed his pants and shorts down to his knees and forced her legs apart. Offended by her actions, when he entered her, he punched her face so hard, he knocked out one of Sandra's front teeth, and the girl at the same time.

When Greg Britton set foot in his office, he felt like he'd never been away. His eyes still stung from all the reading the night before and the months he had taken off were already forgotten. "Where's Mel?" he asked Wally.

"At Sandra's school. I'm just reading her diary. The girl sure didn't like someone by the name of Brentsen.

"Yeah, that's what Holmes said."

"Gaudry passed a phone message to his partner. "As per your instructions, they're dragging the lake and stream this morning."

"Good. Those people are on the ball. Listen, I don't know why, but I think we should look at the bridge and lakeshore again. Bring the diary with you. I'll read it on the way."

Three-quarters-of-an-hour later, the two officers stood looking down from a small bridge crossing a slow flowing stream being whipped up by the wind. In the near distance, the heads of two surfacing frogmen kept breaking the lake's brooding surface. Before heading under again, the rubber-suited professionals spoke with three men and three women sitting in a couple of rowboats and dragging the bottom with grappling hooks.

"I've got a feeling this is a total waste of time," Greg said, putting his collar up and watching the grappling lines striking the water every so often. The wind picked up even more while they watched, and the sky turned to one dark mass of bulging rain clouds ready to burst. To Greg, the clouds looked like two huge black balloons full of water. Whenever they collided, they would cut off what was left of the sun.

"It must be done," Wally said, before inquisitively looking past Greg. A moment later he also said, "I wonder what she wants?"

Britton turned to see a woman across the lake waving her hands trying to attract their attention.

"Let's drive over and find out," Greg said, before waving and yelling, "We'll be right there!"

It only took a few minutes for the two to find the exact house on the lakeshore road, and when they parked their car, a short attractive brown-haired woman came walking towards them. About thirty years old, well proportioned, and wearing a lumberjack shirt and jeans, she asked, "You guys the police?"

"Yeah," Greg said, displaying his badge and following her past her cabin towards her small two-boat wharf. In the distance, both detectives could see the same police dragging activity they had seen from the small wooden bridge. The grapplers didn't look like they could continue much longer because the wind and waves were now on a rampage.

"I'm Lieutenant Greg Britton, and this is my partner Detective Wally Gaudry. And you are...?"

"You mean police officers have first names?" she asked jokingly.

"Yeah, and we also drink coffee," Gaudry remarked, smiling and trying to hide his wince after a penetrating glance from Greg.

The woman also smiled, saying, "I'm Irene Wattelet. Mrs. Irene Wattelet ... divorced. My ex-husband couldn't take my busy way of life or the fact that I earned more money. We're still straightening matters out in court, and next week I hope my name will once again be Irene Tweten. I'm going to get rid of the name Wattelet altogether. I've got some fresh coffee on the stove, but first I would like you to take a look at something."

With the two detectives following, Mrs. Wattelet walked to the water's edge at the side of her wharf where her small boat bounced. There, she pointed to a pair of white jeans snagged on a nail.

"I thought you'd need these," the woman said, handing a plastic garbage bag and a chopstick to Wally who proceeded to delicately remove the garment from the water.

"Thanks, but what's with the chopstick?"

"I couldn't find anything else and I don't believe we're supposed to touch evidence with our hands. Right?" she asked.

"Wally agreed. "Er ... right!"

"Those pants weren't there yesterday," Mrs. Wattelet said. "Could they have belonged to that missing girl?"

"Possibly. Do you live here alone?" Greg asked, peeling his eyes to another object in the water. "Do you have another bag?"

While Mrs. Wattelet walked to her cabin, Wally asked, "What do you think this is?"

"Looks like Sandra's sweater."

After Greg bagged the second clothing article, Mrs. Wattelet ushered the men towards her cottage. "To answer your question, yes, I do live here alone. Not all year 'round though. I bought it as a small summer cottage and I'm taking a few days off work."

"What kind of work do you do?" Wally asked.

"I'm an agent in the film industry."

The two black balloons finally struck each other and burst. As large raindrops began pounding the cabin's roof, the officers and Mrs. Wattelet drank coffee and ate cookies. Soon, the habitual slamming sounds of the rain became very intense and at times drowned out their conversation.

During their talk, it turned out that Mrs. Wattelet hadn't seen anything out of place. After taking all of her particulars, the detectives thanked her, left two cards, and departed.

On the way to their car, Greg chuckled when Wally said, "I should have asked her if her business needs another Dirty Harry."

"You think you could replace Eastwood?"

"Why not?"

"Come off it, Wally … Clint Eastwood doesn't have holes in his socks."

"Hey, it's dark when I get dressed."

"Also, I don't think Clint Eastwood would eat a stranger's cookies? What if they were poisoned?"

"I never turn down chocolate chip cookies. Stranger or no stranger."

"Would you stake your reputation on that?"

"Er … sure, whatever that means?"

"Good, I love Black Angus steak."

After staring incredulously at Greg and being totally ignored, Wally said, "Damn," while getting in the car.

"What was that?" Greg asked, tongue in cheek and hiding his face from his partner.

"Oh, nothing. I guess I'm buying lunch, again," Wally said despondently.

"Yes, and it's most kind of you," Greg said. "You'll not be getting used to this. I like mine well done."

As much as he tried to ignore Wally's downcast expression, when Wally said, "I fucking well hope I won't be getting used to it," Greg couldn't help but to roar out laughing.

On their way to a Black Angus Restaurant, Wally briefed Greg on certain selections from Sandra's diary, and after lunch, the lieutenant scanned the book from cover to cover. When Mel Holmes appeared saying, he'd had no luck finding someone with the name of Brentsen, the team's leader replied, "I don't doubt it. The name's not Brentsen, it's Brantsen. Check it out again. Where's Dabbit?"

"He spent the morning scouring Sandra's house, her yard and the alley as you wanted. Er, an elderly woman across the lane asked if she could speak with him. Her name is…"

"Madge Grant," Greg said, before adding, "Old Madge won't get finished with the poor bastard until midnight. Okay, get back to the school."

"Where are you guys gonna be?" Holmes asked, appearing a bit embarrassed he'd read the name wrong.

"In an hour, Wally and I are going to check out the area where Philip got the flat tire. Keep me posted if you find Brantsen."

"Is it true Philip's parents posted bail," Mel asked.

"Yeah, and it's just as well. We don't believe the kid's involved. In fact, I'll guarantee he's not. That sweater we found at the lake was cut right up the front. He didn't need to do that if all he wanted was to cop a feel."

"That's a crude way of putting it," Wally said, giving Greg an out of place look.

Glancing nonchalantly at his partner, Greg said, "I'm a crude kind of guy."

The rain eased a little as the two detectives parked their car at the end of a middle class residential street and Greg said, "I'll take this side, you take the other."

Most of the houses on the block were built in the forties. By the look of them, each had seen better times. The homeowner of the first house Britton approached indicated he may have seen the youth in the photo, but moments later he changed his mind.

Across the street, Wally thought he might be having a little luck when a woman with a baby in her arms indicated she recognized the car and called her husband. Unfortunately, she had second thoughts, and her husband just shook his head.

While Wally had difficulty moving a St. Bernard's paws off his chest, and dribble from the dog's jowls from his coat, suit jacket and the front of his pants, a teenage boy across the street expressed some interest before shaking his head negatively to Greg.

After managing to get the dog down, Gaudry closed the gate and fully entered the front yard of the green wooden house. Trying to erase the large amount of slime with a handkerchief just spread the snail-trail-like discharge and concern showed on the detective's face. He was still trying to clean off his pants while he walked up the stairs and rang the doorbell. Not receiving an answer, he turned and was halfway down the stairs towards more wagging tail and additional drool when the door opened.

"Can I help you, young man?" a smiling, libidinous-looking woman asked, wearing a tight purple cotton dress, black nylons, and frayed yellow slippers. Playing with her dazzling red wig and pressing her recently lipsticked fire engine red lips together, the heavy pensioner presented Wally with an inviting look and said, "I'm Miss. Bonita-Thelma Figaro. If President Clinton likes you, I like you."

"Uh, President Clinton?"

"My St. Bernard. Those are his paw prints on your clothes, aren't they? He leaves his prints on dresses as well."

Wally Gaudry caught the joke and smiled going through his routine. Moments later after he whistled for Greg to come over, he noticed President Clinton didn't bother the lieutenant.

"Er, Greg, this is Mrs. Figarello. She…"

"It's Figaro … Miss Bonita-Thelma Figaro," the woman said, appearing like a lost little girl and flapping her black caked eyelashes at both officers. "Please call me Bonita-Thelma."

Smiling and nodding apologetically, Wally cleared his throat. "Sorry about that. Uh, Greg … Miss. Figaro saw Phillip and…"

"No, Detective Wally. It's Bonita-Thelma," the woman repeated, blinking and smiling seductively at the officer. My grandfather was a sailing ship captain, and he married my grandma who was Bonita-Thelma. Both my mother and me were named after her."

"How charming," Greg offered, wincing at the mud and huge amount of slobber covering the front of Gaudry's clothes. Smiling at his partner's tedious expression, he said, "We're police officers, Bonita Thelma. I'm Greg Britton and this is Wally Gaudry."

"Yes I know. Detective Wally's introduced himself. Such a lovely name …Wally. That's short for Walter isn't it?"

Wally finally stretched his lips, bared some teeth and repaid the compliment, saying, "Yes, it is. You also have such lovely names, Bonita Thelma. Uh, Miss Bonita saw…"

"Bonita-Thelma, please," the woman said, maintaining the same blameless smiling facial expression made famous by Britain's late Queen Mother Elizabeth when she waved to a crowd.

"Er, Bonita-Thelma here thinks she saw Philip fix his tire. Uh, isn't that right, Bonita-Thelma?"

"Yes I surely did see him," the woman said, allowing her upper right arm's dangling flab to sway as she raised it pointing to the opposite side of the street. I'm also the leader of our neighbourhood watch. My best friend, Hilda-May Biddlecombe is…"

"How nice," Greg said, trying to stick to the facts. "Er, can you point out exactly where the young man stood when he fixed his tire?"

"I just did … right over there," Miss. Figaro said, pointing across the street again. "Right there on the other side. That's exactly where he was."

"How long was he there?" Wally asked, still maintaining his stretched cheeks resembling an open-mouthed smile.

"About twenty minutes, and it was raining cats and dogs," the woman replied as her right leg's stocking fell to her ankle. Turning towards Wally and sensuously lifting up the hem of her dress, she rolled the black nylon above her knee and tied a knot. Grinning bashfully, she said, "I also have a cat named Monica, and sometimes when it rains I say it's raining Clintons and Lewinskys. Do you think that's foolish of me, Detective Wally?"

"It figures," Greg muttered, making notes before looking up and grinning. "What time did he pull over?"

The woman ignored Greg and kept her eyes on Wally.

"No, not at all, Bonita-Thelma. In fact, it's rather cute."

"Like me?" she asked, flapping her eyelashes.

"Uh, yes, just like you."

"What a lovely name … Wally. My Monica is such a rebellious little cat. Her self-assurance reminds me so much of me when I was young. Oh, I drove the boys wild. Still do, actually, and people say I am most young looking for my age. What do you think, Detective Wally?"

Wally now knew the routine. "I've been asking myself that question and I'd say you're either thirty-three or thirty-four. If I'm over, please tell me."

Greg thought if Wally had sold life insurance, the woman would have bought at least ten policies.

Instantly, Bonita Thelma moved next to the young detective and gave him a hip check. "Oh, Walter, you sweet wonderful boy, you. We could make wonderful music together. Did I tell you I took dancing lessons and I..."

"What time did he pull over?" Greg asked.

"Wally is such a lovely name," Miss Figaro said, now grabbing the upper left arm of Wally's raincoat and yanking him closer to her. You remind me of the first boy that captured my heart. What a naughty boy Bertram was. Do you like to be called Walter or Wally?"

"It doesn't matter. Er, what time did he pull over?"

"It was about twelve-thirty. See, I have a wonderful memory, don't I, Policeman Wally. Hilda-May Biddlecombe tells me to make notes, so I do. She was an air raid warden during the Korean War, and..."

"That's really interesting. Are you absolutely certain of the time, Bonita-Thelma?" Greg asked, oozing milk and honey.

After impatiently glancing at Greg and saying, "I certainly am because I make notes, the woman returned her attention to Gaudry. "Many say that I have the memory of an eighteen year old. Some would even say the body of an eighteen year old as well. It was about twelve-thirty. Anyway, he was such a naughty, naughty boy."

The "naughty" part instantly aroused Greg's interest. "Really? Why, what did he do?"

Blushing, Miss Figaro said, "Not many people ask me that and I don't know if I should tell you ... but Harvey always lifted up my petticoat and..."

"No, no, not Harvey, Miss ... uh, Bonita Thelma, we're talking about Philip Bayer. What did he do?"

"Oh, him ... yes. Well, after the girl got out, she kissed him on his left cheek and began quickly walking towards Maple Street. Say, I've just baked two big apple pies. Would you boys like to come in and try out my pies? C'mon, Wally, you look like you need to put some meat on those nice-looking bones?"

Wally and Greg pleasantly glanced at each other before the lieutenant said, "No, thank you. He's an anthropophagite, and I'm on a diet. Can you remember anything else?"

Still fluttering her massive eye lashes, Bonita Thelma said, "No, not really. I have two rhubarb pies in the oven, Detective Wally. Would you like to take a pie with you?"

Wally found himself wincing and scratching his head. "Thank you anyway, Bonita-Thelma. Which direction did he take when he drove away?"

"He pulled a U-turn and drove the other way, towards Birch Street. Like I said, it was really raining, and I bet he got drenched fixing that tire. When I get that wet, I take a nice long warm shower; but I don't really like showering alone if you know what I mean. Do you shower alone ... Wally?"

"Uh, yes I do, Bonita-Thelma."

"Really? Well I like to gyrate in the shower, and..."

Wally's body language pleaded with Greg to terminate the prism of mutual *adoration*. "Miss, er, Bonita-Thelma, you're an enormously observant and talented young lady, and we thank you for helping us. Here's my card if you think of anything else, please give me a call."

Miss. Figaro's come-on look heightened then quickly waned and she pouted a little. "I'd like Detective Wally's card too, please."

After thanking the woman and handing her his card, Wally was halfway down the stairs when Miss. Figaro said, "Hilda-May Biddlecombe's taking criminology at night school. Er, Detective Wally, did I tell you I'm unattached and looking."

Gaudry's cheeks stretched again as he turned and waved before maintaining the same frozen mouth while whispering to Greg, "I'm not, thank God."

"Bonita-Thelma's got the hots for ya," the elder of the two said, heading to their car. "Why didn'tcha get in there and have a taste of her pies?"

Wally kept his head and eyes to his front. "No thanks. I've got a feeling she wanted me to taste a hellova lot more than her pies. By the way, what's an anthrop … er, an anthropophagite?"

"I think it means you're strictly a meat eater. Either that or you're a cannibal."

"A cannibal? Like eating human flesh and all that?"

"Exactly."

"Jesus, thanks, Greg. I think that's what the woman wanted."

Greg's belly laugh started Wally laughing, and the duo wondered how they could find humour in the midst of this dreadful puzzle.

Nearing their car, Britton said, "The captain will want to hear about this."

A questioning look came over Wally's face. "The captain? Why the captain?"

"He likes rhubarb pie. For that matter, any kind of pie."

"Hey, yeah, they're made for each other. Let's hook 'em up."

Finding humour in the midst of this dreadful puzzle kept the detectives on track. Greg smacked Wally's back. "Nah, it wouldn't be fair. She'd rather have you."

"Forget it. I like sweet potato pie."

"I'll bet she would make you sweet potato pie or any other kind of pie. Want me to ask her?"

Still feeling embarrassed and trying not to laugh while getting in the car, Wally said, "Gimmee a break, Greg."

A ringing cellular took the senior police officer's mind off the words to an old British children's poem. Four and Twenty Blackbirds Baked in a Pie.

"Britton."

"Lieutenant, it's Allan Dabbit."

"Hello Al. I understand you're busy keeping Madge Grant happy?"

"Hey, she's a nice old broad. Over a beer, she tried to convince me to join her church, and she wants my wife to join the Daughters of the American Revolution. Madge is the past president of this area's chapter."

Britton cocked his head and winked at Wally. "Oh, so you're on a first name basis now, eh? I think Mrs. Grant will be good for the both of you. What have you got?"

"A page from Sandra's homework with blood on it. There's also blood on the ground where Madge found it."

Greg sat up straight. "One page?"

"Yeah."

"Is it fingerprint blood?"

"No, just a clot."

"Where's the rest of the blood?"

"On the ground on the right side of Madge's garage ... out of her sight and just under the eaves. She found the page this morning. I think the wind blew it there and it caught on something."

Greg hesitated, thinking about the layout of Madge's lot. "Facing Madge's house from the alley, there's a fence on the left side with about two feet between that fence and her garage. An end piece attaches the fence to her garage. Was the blood in the actual alley or just behind the end fence?"

"Behind the fence. From the amount of blood, I'd say someone opened a vein in Madge's yard. I've sent three samples to the lab, plus the page."

"Good. Any footprints?"

"No, like every other area I've searched, if there were any, they've been washed away."

For some reason Greg couldn't get the poem *Four and Twenty Blackbirds*, out of his mind when he asked, "Al, have you heard from Holmes?"

"Yeah, he's been back at her school now checking out all of Sandra's haunts again. He says if this guy Brantsen exists, he'll find him."

"Okay. What are your plans?"

"I'm going over everything in Sandra's house one more time."

"Good, keep me posted."

Greg Britton didn't go home that afternoon. Instead, when Wally dropped him off at the police station, the lieutenant searched the main computer's archived files for anything his department had on the Everton rapist his son Jeff had mentioned. Information was scanty about the Everton cases, but something else caught the detective's attention. Three years after the Everton rapes, similar assaults had taken place in Mount Coux, Washington. Eight rape cases had been reported, and a girl had disappeared just before a cardboard box containing ten pairs of soiled panties was found outside a local abortion clinic.

Sitting at a computer, Greg found himself muttering, "He kills before he moves on, and for some insane reason he gloats about his triumphs by leaving souvenirs from the girls he's raped."

Driving home that night, Greg's mind roamed constantly about Everton, Mount Coux, and about Four and Twenty Blackbirds Baked in a Pie.

Chapter 7

The sun's early morning rays once again fought hard to break through the dark overcast, and the four detectives driving towards the mine's entrance knew the fireball's light was facing a losing battle - rain wasn't far off.

"So no Brantsen?" Greg asked his colleague Mel Holmes, before getting out of the car.

"That's right, Lieutenant, no Brantsen. I guess I've spoken to at least three hundred students and all of Sandra's schoolteachers, and no one's heard the name."

Just as they got out of their car, a middle-aged man who had been pulling boards off the mine entrance a few minutes earlier came over to meet them. Around forty and tall, he wore hard-toed work boots, black coveralls and a baseball cap. Greg noticed the State Parks and Recreation logos on the cap and coveralls were coming loose, and both needed some stitching. The lieutenant also observed an identical logo on the man's dark green pickup truck. "I'm Greg Britton," he said, holding out his hand.

Shaking the offered hand, the tall thin man with a pointed nose replied, "Hank Dabchick." "You the officer that called?"

After nodding and introducing the three other officers, Greg said, "You'll probably forget our names … I know I do when I'm introduced to four people, so we'll leave our cards with you. Er, who else has access to this mine?"

"Just me," Dabchick said, making curious eye contact with each of them. "We won't be using the elevators; I don't think they're safe enough. What's this about?"

Hank Dabchick had kind eyes and Greg liked the man. "Worked here long, Hank?"

"About seven years. Are all you police officers planning on going down?"

"Yeah, we wanna take a good look down there. Is it accessible?" Wally asked.

Greg noticed Hank's thinning hair when the man took his cap off to rub his forehead.

"Sure," Dabchick said. "I can't see any reason why not. There are four quarter mile tunnels, startin' at seventy feet. The air's bad, so I gotta start the old pump. I can't let you down if it don't turn over."

Greg understood. "That's fine."

"Four quarter mile tunnels?" Wally asked, accepting a photocopy sketch of the burrows below.

"Yeah, four quarter mile tunnels. There are miners' hats and coveralls in the back of my truck. Although the hats have lights, each of you should also take a Big Bertha lamp and hook it to your coveralls. Also, grab a communicator."

Hank Dabchick attempted starting the pump motor while the detectives got dressed. It took the supervisor a few tries getting the old pump motor to catch and when it did, each police officer heard the loud constant beating swish of giant bellows somewhere within fifty yards. They wouldn't hear the pump when they were below ground.

While Greg got into his pair of coveralls, Dabchick came over. "I think we should give it a good half-hour before we enter.

Britton grinned cordially and nodded. "Any rooms down there, Hank?"

Dabchick casually rolled a cigarette and lit up. "A few ... the miners used 'em. No one in his or her right mind would be down there now. What are you officers lookin' for?"

"We don't know yet," Greg said, pulling on his coveralls.

Wally asked, "Anything we should be aware of while we're down there? Like, er, bugs, bats, rats, uh, snakes?"

"Nah, but the ladders are not in the best of shape. I'll take a hammer and nails and check 'em out ahead of you guys."

Forty minutes later when the wind picked up and rain began thrashing the area, Hank Dabchick covered up the back of his truck with a red tarpaulin and said, "Turn on your cap lights. Everyone ready?"

The four officers obeyed and followed the parks employee to the entrance.

"There are seven ladders to the mine level, and small ledges at the bottom of each ladder. When you reach the mud landing ledges, shuffle around and feel for the next ladder. Watch your step. Only one person should use a ladder at a time. I'll head down and yell up when the next one should start, and then each of you can do the same. Okay?"

"Sounds good," Holmes said, shrugging to his fellow officers. "Hey, boss ... we got insurance for doin' this stuff?"

Grinning, Britton didn't answer his subordinate. The lieutenant was too interested in watching the mine manager disappear. About two minutes later after he heard hammering, he heard Dabchick's faint echoic voice say, "Okay, I'm heading down the next ladder ... the first person can start."

Greg climbed down and disappeared. In about a minute as he shuffled around a small slippery ledge to find the next ladder, he yelled, "Okay, Wally, come on down. He also listened to the instructions coming up from Hank Dabchick."

"Christ, these ladders sound and feel like they could collapse at any minute," Greg muttered, hugging the wooden ladders and slowly shuffling his feet around the sticky ledges at each landing.

At certain spots water oozed from the walls, soaking the ladder braces and the officer wondered how the wooden contraptions stayed attached to the walls. Above, he could hear the faint voices of his crew and he kept Wally advised when to start. "Okay Wally, I'm heading down the next one now, and if I catch the prick we're looking for, I'm gonna break his neck for putting me through this."

Greg heard Wally's faint voice saying, "Same here," before repeating the go-ahead instructions. "Okay, Mel…"

Fifteen minutes later, Dabchick yelled, "Hold it up for a sec while I hammer in a nail. Also, the sixth rung is missing. Advise the others."

Greg began feeling the lower temperature and could see his breath as he descended deeper into the chamber of *indistinct echoes*. He knew he was nearing the bottom when a light lit up his legs and he climbed down into a large clearing with more than ample headroom.

"That wasn't so bad, was it?" Dabchick asked, grinning while standing at the bottom of the ladder and using his Big-Bertha light to guide Greg down.

"No, not at all," the lieutenant said noticing four individually numbered ten-foot wide by seven-foot high tunnels leading away from the centre area were they stood. "Although I'm not exactly relishing the thought of climbing back up. Say, if we didn't have these lights it would be pitch black."

Dabchick chuckled. "Even a cat couldn't see in here, Lieutenant. There is no light in this particular area whatsoever. Would you mind telling me what you're looking for?"

"I can't right now, Hank. Uh, is it always this cool?"

"Yeah, and it gets colder in the shafts."

A few moments later Wally's feet emerged and in similar timed intervals, Holmes and Dabbit followed him.

"Turn on your Big-Berthas," Dabchick told, them before asking, "Who is the youngest?"

"It's me," Greg said, trying to keep a straight face. "I just look older than them."

The remark lit up Dabchick's firm face and Greg received a few off the ball comments from his co-workers before Dabbit offered, "I think it's me."

"Okay, er, you come with me, and we'll take Tunnel One. You other three, the routes are marked on your maps."

Greg checked his map. "I'll take Two. Wally, you take Three, and Mel … you take Four. Check out all rooms and offshoots, and anything that looks, *interesting*."

Examining their drawings, the police officers motioned they understood.

"You'll come across pools of crystal clear water," Dabchick said. "It's drinkable. Probably the best water you'll ever taste. Should be bottled."

Dabbit's teeth began chattering. "Christ, I'm freezing … I won't be drinking any water."

Edging Dabbit to the first tunnel the mine supervisor said, "Er, stay in your own tunnels. You will see ore offshoots … most are dead ends or they just pull u-turns and lead back to the main tunnels."

"Any rooms in the offshoots?" Greg asked, now feeling the cold Dabbit mentioned.

"No."

Greg headed away, saying, "Okay, let's get this over with."

The lieutenant didn't rush examining his tunnel, and his ears and nerves never became accustomed to the eerie sounds his burrow gradually emitted. Faint musical wind sounds came from every direction, along with dripping water, his beating heart, his footsteps, and the fading distant incoherent echoing voices of the other four men.

Along the way, Greg passed beautiful clear pools of water; small lagoons kids would die for on hot summer days. "Hell, not just kids … even me," he mumbled.

With his miners' headlight and Big-Bertha guiding the way, Greg Britton's beams explored the walls, ceilings, smooth hard-packed dirt floors and the strong wooden support braces holding the mine together. For the first time in a long while he felt alone in this strange clay universe and his thoughts centred on those "poor souls" that had been buried alive in the old days.

"Light a fire in this hell hole and the devil would move in," he muttered, wishing this part of his investigation was over with.

After walking around a ninety-degree corner, Greg entered the first room off his tunnel. A four-foot square table made out of rough lumber stood in the middle of the large chamber. Miners had carved their initials all over it, and similar old wooden bunk beds standing nearby. The bunks were stacked five high and covered two walls. The officer's Big-Bertha discovered the room's wiring and an ancient light bulb jutting from a fixture attached to the dirt ceiling had Greg muttering, "If that thing lasted all these years, General Electric should tell the world."

Before continuing on his route, the lieutenant checked his map to see if the room was indicated. It was, and he felt better knowing his location. Overconfidence, however, didn't prepare him for the cat's tail he stepped on re-entering the tunnel, nor could confidence have trained his heart from jumping out of his chest when the animal's screech sent him flying backwards, hitting the wall, buckling his knees and landing on his buttocks.

With goose bumps forming that could have emblazoned his name in the Guinness Book of Records, Greg's yell would have indeed scared the devil had the archfiend moved in. "Christ! What the…?"

Realizing his situation and getting up quickly, the officer mouthed, "Thank God I haven't got a pacemaker. I'll probably need one after this. Where in hell did that cat come from? Dabchick said even cats couldn't see down here."

Not far ahead, Greg found out the answer to his question when he mouthed, "Daylight and fresh air? Down here?"

Viewing dim light appearing from around the next bend, the officer thought he must have been hallucinating. A moment later he mumbled, "How can there be daylight and fresh air seven stories below the surface?"

Silently staying to the left side of the tunnel, Greg slowed his pace and fifty feet ahead, he saw bright daylight coming through a thick iron-mesh gate next to a room entrance similar to the one he had just left.

Creeping into the room, the curious but cautious officer's eyes widened. The chamber was about the same size as the last room, and it held the usual bunk beds and table, but it was also *furnished*. Clothes littered a chair, and pairs of dirty boots and sneakers had been neatly placed together against one wall. A sleeping bag and some old tattered blankets covered a lower bunk, and a bucket of water, clean eating utensils, and a tin plate and cup sat in the middle of the table.

Greg scoured the room with his Big-Bertha light. To feel the Coleman stove and kerosene lantern, he had to duck under a rope clothesline holding two pairs of off-coloured once white long johns. Both Coleman items were warm indicating someone had recently been in the room.

"The cat's screech and my howl probably scared the bastard," the lieutenant muttered.

Concern covered the police officer's face as he studied the steel gate at the end of his tunnel. Greg had arrived at some kind of an ore-dumping shoot on the other side of the mountain high above the floor of the gravel pit. He thought miners must have tilted their ore carts here, jettisoning the mineral-bearing rock down a wooden slide that had probably rotted away decades ago.

The surrounding outdoor area was just as quiet as the tunnel, except for the drumming rain and the sound of squawking crows. Straining his eyes, he could see the distant black birds circling the quarry where he had gone to find Sandra and Philip on the night of her disappearance. No cars were parked with necking lovers; it was barren and alone just like it had been that night.

Greg was just about to turn and reinvestigate the room when he noticed the gate's lock wasn't clamped. It was in its proper position, holding the gate to its frame, but it remained open.

Taking the lock off and pulling the squeaking gate towards him, the police officer arrived at the conclusion it would be impossible to climb down, therefore whoever used the entrance had gone up.

Holding on to the frame and turning his head so he could look up and to his right, Greg heard a few pebbles rolling down the ledge from the area left of the gate. Moving over and straining his neck upwards, he saw the legs of a crouching male form.

With his heart pounding and every hair on end, Britton reached up and around, grabbing the front of the man's work shirt, before hauling him in. "C'mere you son-of-a-bitch," he yelled, determinedly smashing the man against an inner tunnel wall and getting ready to hit him.

"Mister, I ain't done nothin' wrong," the old man insisted, expressing a nervous facial twitch and cowering. "I ain't hurt anyone. I mind my own business. Mister, I ain't done nothin' wrong."

When the officer released his grip, the trembling five-foot-eight old man with missing teeth, a dirty white beard, full head of white hair, stained clothes and an unstable facial twitch slid down the wall and sat on the floor, legs extended. "I ain't never hurt a fly since the war. I mind my own business."

A bit of Greg's composure returned. "Who the hell are you, and what are you doing here?"

Not realizing the scared man couldn't catch his breath to reply, Greg bent and grabbed the front of the man's shirt again. "Quickly, or so help me I'm gonna…"

"I'm, I'm Art … Arthur the hobo. I'm only Art the hobo. I don't bother no one, Mister."

"What are you doing in here?"

"Live here … yeah, I live here. I don't bother no one. I ain't never hurt anyone since the war … I'm Art the hobo."

Confused, Greg knelt next to the man. "You actually live in this rat hole?"

A small appreciative weather-beaten smile appeared and the old man's blue eyes glistened. "Since I got home from the wars. Don't tell no one."

Not too certain of the man's age, Greg asked, "What wars?"

"Korea and Vietnam. I tried to join before but they got wise to my age. Also, there ain't no rats here, General Patton takes care of 'em."

"General Patton?"

"My cat. I think you met the general."

Grinning, Greg helped the radiant eyed old man to his feet. "Yeah, he scared the living shit outta me."

When Art cackled, only one upper tooth appeared. "The general's my buddy. We stay away from trouble."

Britton took the communicator out of his coveralls pocket. "Hey, Hank … I got company here."

"Company?" Dabchick asked, before saying, "Oh, you've met Art? I forgot to tell you about Art the hobo."

Art chuckled lowly when Greg said, "Nice to be warned, Hank. A few minutes ago I thought I'd need a heart transplant."

Laughing, Dabchick said, "Art's harmless. I let him stay here and he keeps me informed."

"About what?"

"People hangin' around. He's okay … just leave him be."

After Greg put his walkie-talkie away, he said, "Sorry about that, Art. Are you okay?"

Art indicated he was fine. "I stay to myself. It's better this way 'cause I've seen all the brutal acts I didn't wanna see in the first place."

Reaching through his coveralls and taking out his wallet, Greg smiled sympathetically while handing a twenty-dollar bill to the old timer. "Yes, you probably have. I'm sorry I bothered you, sir. Good luck to you and General Patton."

Art's eyes grew brighter viewing the twenty in his hand. "Wow, many thanks … thankee."

After turning to leave, the lieutenant faced the old man again. "Anyone else live here, Art?"

Art shook his head. "No."

"Have you seen people hanging around the quarry lately?"

"Just kids. I watch 'em from up here. They drink then break their bottles. I don't bother no one."

"Anything else? Like, er … did you see a kid dropping a jacket on a bush or the ground?"

Again, Art indicated he hadn't.

"Well, thanks, Art. Good luck to you."

After walking a few steps, Greg heard, "Not a kid … it was a man."

Turning quickly, Greg asked, "Who wasn't a kid? Art, did you see someone throwing a windbreaker onto a bush?"

"Yeah."

"What did he look like? Did he have a vehicle?"

"Couldn't tell … too high to see. Besides, I don't bother no one."

The warm squad room felt good as Greg Britton smiled thinking of his encounter the day before with Art the hobo. "Where's the old geezer now?" he asked Wally.

"With our artist."

"Okay, drive him back when she's finished with him and give him this twenty."

"Greg, you gave him twenty yesterday," Wally said, adding, "You should be keeping that money for lunches."

Britton had to turn his head away. "I don't need it for lunches … you always insist on buying. Besides, I kinda like him."

Wally's incredulous look turned into a slight unbelieving grin, but Greg's face remained unchanged, so the detective didn't know if his boss was serious or not.

The four detectives had arrived at their office early, all eagerly awaiting the lab report on the homework page and the blood found behind Madge's house.

After taking off his jacket and loosening his tie, Greg sat at his desk and rolled up his sleeves. "Allan, Mel, I want soil samples taken where those garments were found at the lake.

"Check," Holmes replied, pouring two coffees. "We've just got some paperwork to catch up on then we'll be on our way."

"Fine. Oh, yeah, and Wally, when you drive Art back, get some soil samples from around the mine entrance. Also take a damned good look at the area where the jacket was found and estimate what you think Art could see from that distance."

"What are you gonna do?" Wally asked, putting on his raincoat.

"I'll be here. I read those files and something's missing. Oh, and Wally, take soil samples from the alley outside Sandra's back gate, Madge's garage, and from Gosling's backyard. Okay?"

"Do you think she's still alive?" Dabbit asked Greg.

Britton put on his glasses and opened the first file. "Yeah, she's alive, but I don't think there's much time left. This son of a bitch kills before he moves on. Beforehand though, he leaves *testimonials.*"

The three other faces appeared confused.

"It's just a hunch and I'll explain later," Greg said, checking his watch that read eight-thirty. "Now, let's get this show on the road."

Three hours later, Greg sat alone at his desk reading the files when he picked up his phone and punched out three numbers.

"It's Greg Britton, is Ray there? Yeah, I'll wait."

With his phone still to his ear, the lieutenant continued reading for about fifteen seconds until he heard a response. "Ray, it's Greg Britton; how ya doin? Good. Yeah, it's getting easier, thanks. Uh, when you checked Sandra Potts' shoes and jacket, what else did you find?" Making notes, Greg said, "Uh huh, okay. Er, recheck the jacket, the shoes and the homework papers found at the lake. See if you missed anything. Yeah, yeah, I know your people never miss things, but hell, we're all human, ain't we? Okay, okay, I agree ... you're not human. Actually, I'll tell ya a secret. Most guys in this department think you're a goddamned alien."

Chuckling, Greg held the phone away from his ear, but people nearby couldn't mistake the words, "Screw them!" emanating from the earpiece.

"Listen, the file says our rapist has 0-positive blood. What type of blood does Sandra have? What type is that ... A-positive? Good, thanks Ray. Anything new on that homework page and the blood found outside Madge Grant's garage? Soon, eh? What about Sandra's jeans and sweater? Jesus, Ray, how about you and your staff giving up the coffee and doughnuts and doing some work?" An attentive smile came to his lips. "Yeah, and same to you. Good, I'll be here."

After placing the phone down and picking up a pencil, when the lieutenant opened a file, his lips mouthed, "Sing a song of sixpence, a pocket full of rye. Four and twenty blackbirds baked in a..." The senior police officer slammed the pencil against open file's papers and sat back, muttering, "Why the hell am I thinking about blackbirds again? So Sandy liked birds ... so what?"

Greg Britton never chewed his nails, but this time he found his teeth discovering the top part of his right thumbnail as his gazing inquisitive eyes inadvertently glued themselves to anything moving in the office. He asked himself if he could be thinking about blackbirds because of the crows at the mine, or was it because the pie lady had the hots for Wally.

"Nah, it's not Bonita Banana or whatever the hell her name is. There are crows everywhere. What about the bird pictures on the girl's wallpaper, or her bedspread? Yeah, she had pictures of birds everywhere; why am I so interested in them? Am I interested in birds? I must be because I can't get that goddamned rhyme out of my ... wait a minute, yes wait a minute. Her diary was found under her mattress. A mattress covered by sheets, pillows, and a bedspread depicting various birds.

Standing in a hurry and picking up his phone again, Greg thought, Britton you're a genius. There's no person named Brantsen. A Brant is a wild goose and that's what Sandra used as a codeword for Gosling. Nearly placing the talking end of his cellular into his mouth, he yelled, "Wally where the hell are ya?"

"Hold on a sec," Wally replied, before saying, "Art, here's another twenty dollars from the lieutenant. He says to thank you for your assistance."

Greg Britton heard the old hobo replying, "Thankee, much appreciated. Thank him and tell him I don't bother no one."

"Yeah, we know that. Thanks again. What's up, Greg?"

"A Brant is a goose ... that's what's up."

After a short pause, Wally didn't have to be told the second time. "Shit, yeah. So she used that term in case someone found her diary."

"You got it," Britton said standing up in a hurry. "I'm getting a search warrant. How long will it take you to get here?"

"About forty minutes."

"Good. Meet me behind my house in an hour. We're gonna pick up that son of a bitch."

Captain Sam Csontos arrived at Greg's desk just as the lieutenant finished speaking with his partner.

"From your excitement, I'd say you've got something?" Sam asked.

Greg rolled down his sleeves and put on his tie. "Remember I mentioned Sandra was being followed … that the same guy kept turning up wherever she was?"

"Yeah."

"I think it was Gosling. That bastard gets out somehow."

Sam's forehead crinkled. "But he's a fucking vegetable? He hasn't got enough sense to know what he's doing."

"How do we know that?" Greg asked, putting on his suit jacket. "I've never spoken with him, and neither have you."

Rain was again the order of the day when two police cars arrived at the front of the Gosling house and two police cars parked in the alley. At exactly the same time as Greg pounded on the back door, Wally Gaudry stood by the lower basement back door and Dabbit and Holmes covered the front entrance. Four uniformed police officers covered the alley and the front of the house and street.

"Open the door, Vernon, or we'll have to damage it coming in." Greg yelled, holding a two-foot long piece of two-by-four wood and pounding as hard as he could.

A lengthy thirty seconds went by before Britton heard the bolts slowly being pulled back and the door opening its usual three inches.

"Why the fuck don't you assholes leave us alone?" the elder Gosling mouthed standing directly behind the door.

Greg displayed the warrant. "Get the chain off and open up, Vernon; I've got a search warrant."

As Gosling tried to shut the door, shouting, "I don't give a fuck what you've got, you ain't comin' in here," Greg shoved the plank in at the bottom of the door to keep it open. Then turning his right side towards the entry and using his full weight, the police lieutenant ploughed through the barrier like a swinging wrecking ball. Breaking the lock and forcing the entrance wide open, Greg's action thrust Vernon Gosling backwards towards an old wood-burning kitchen stove.

Dressed only in dirty blue jeans and throatily offering every swear word he'd ever used, Gosling quickly picked up a piece of firewood, and came at Greg with the determined ferocity of a lion at killing time. Unfortunately, this lion wasn't about to eat. Greg had grabbed hold of the two-by-four off the floor and that item stopped the forward downward motion of Gosling's wooden weapon. Next, Britton's gloved right fist slammed into the middle of the threatening man's face sending him flying back against the stove before folding up in front of it like a baby in the foetal position.

"Cuff that son-of-a-bitch to the stove," Greg said to Wally rushing in on the scene. "I'm through being nice with that bastard."

"I can see that," Gaudry offered, turning the senior Gosling on his stomach, frisking the man's pants, and attaching the cuffs to Gosling's right wrist and the oven door's handle. "Jesus, this guy has really cut his right hand. Look at this, Greg. It's been neatly sewn up."

"Yeah, I saw the stitches."

Except for the repulsive odour of stale body sweat, Greg thought the interior of the house wasn't as bad as the outside. Walking through the living room to open the front door, he thought the place needed cleaning, but he arrived at the conclusion he'd seen worse joints when their owners had become head cases. The interior layout of the house was the same as his house, but the furniture was older and the house's accoutrements appeared European. Two walls in the living room held small Turkish rugs and tapestries, and three small alcoves built into the other walls held framed photographs of what Greg assumed was an Eastern European farming family or a gathering of villagers.

"Okay, Ronnie Gosling's in here someplace and I'm not certain what mood he's in, Greg said in the living room. "If he uses a butcher knife to kill mosquitoes, I wonder what he'd like to use on us. Allan Mel, check the basement and be careful. I'll take this floor. Wally, you're gonna love me for this. There's a ladder behind the stove. Use it to climb up and search the attic. The ceiling entrance is left of the stove, and you'll find a light switch on the wall. The roof's just high enough for you to walk around up there, but keep your head down and your eyes peeled."

"How do you know all this? Wally asked.

"This house is identical to mine; built by the same contractor. I added a back porch and front concrete stairs."

Over the next forty minutes, the police lieutenant thought he might have been premature in judging the inhabitants' lifestyle. The two main bedrooms and the guest bedroom were a shambles. Dirty clothes and footwear were strewn everywhere and Greg knew the sheets hadn't been washed in months. In the master bedroom where the old man slept, the bedclothes were covered in dried blood and dirt. It appeared Vernon Gosling usually went to bed with his boots on.

An hour later when Captain Sam Csontos arrived, Doctor Ronald Gosling had not been found.

MANIAC

Chapter 8

Okay, you have a lot of explaining to do, Vernon, so let's quit the bullshit. I'm asking you again … where are they?"

"Who?"

A frustrated look ensnared Greg Britton's face. "Your son and Sandra Potts. Don't give me the 'Who' shit, Gosling."

"Just because that hussy's missin', my son's supposed to have her? You're a fuckin' riot, Britton, you really are. All you cops are fuckin' fruitcakes compared to my Ronnie. You think he's sick? Hell, let me tell you somethin' you thick-headed prick, he's got more brains than the bunch of you fuckers combined."

Two hours after arresting Vernon Gosling, the sinewy man with the half-closed left eye wasn't about to reveal anything. Conducting a thorough search of his house also came up dry.

"What are you so mad at the world for, Vernon? Are you pissed off because little Ronnie isn't the state's hero anymore?

Or are you pissed off because you know we're getting closer to nailing him with those murder charges?"

"What murder charges? What the fuck are you talkin' about, Britton?"

"You've been spending too much time with your cuckoo son, Vernon," Greg said, rubbing it in and leaning across the table. "You're getting like him - a total head case."

Old man Gosling stood up fast and raised his right hand before feeling the back of Greg's right hand across his face, forcing him to fall backwards over his chair, spread-eagled on the floor.

Greg stood over him. "Do that again and I'll forget what being nice means. Where are they?"

Gosling didn't say a word as Wally helped him up to his chair. For a quick moment, Greg thought the man wanted to say something, but hatred arrived just as quickly. "Go fuck yourself, Britton."

"Why is your hand cut to pieces?" Wally asked.

Rapidly following Wally's question, Greg asked, "Yeah, what happened to your hand, Vernon? Did your maniac son find a mosquito on it? Did he? Or did your maniac son find you trying to change his diaper and he didn't like it?"

The old man's eyes turned to fire and he clenched his hands together so tightly, numerous stitches parted on his right hand and blood oozed from his palm.

"Do it, Gosling … go on! Just raise your hand at me one more time," Greg said. "Where are they? Where's your maniac son, Gosling? Where's that so-called proud member of the insane society?"

In what seemed like slow motion, Greg watched and listened as Gosling's eyes and mouth exploded and the screaming man leaned over the table with the ferocity of a bull elephant. He was quick because Britton couldn't get out of his way fast enough and Gosling grabbed the officer by his shirt and tie, pulled him closer and head butted him. A fraction of a second later the raging bull turned his attention to take care of Gaudry, but this time he wasn't quick enough because Wally hit the blaring man's face with the glass bottom of the table's heavy water jug, knocking him out cold.

"Are you okay?" Wally asked, placing cuffs on Gosling and watching Greg stand and feel his nose and forehead. Although there was a small cut above Greg's right eye, the majority of the blood covering the front of the lieutenant's shirt belonged to Gosling.

"It could have been worse," Greg said, wiping blood from his nose. "I managed to back off just as he made contact. I must be getting slow. I knew the bastard was going to make a move, but I didn't react quickly enough."

"Must be all those free lunches," Gaudry said, casually picking up the second full water jug and dumping the iced liquid over the head of the now moaning man writhing on the floor. "You need to go on a diet, Greg."

Greg didn't bother replying, but after realizing Wally delivered the line with a straight face, he knew the kid was learning. Yeah, a bit of the senior echelon was rubbing off on the youthful detective after all, he thought.

Gaudry finally got Gosling to his feet and after pushing him back into his chair, asked, "Well, what are we going to do with this prick now?"

"We're going to stay with him until he cracks," Greg replied. "Go get us a couple of coffees."

"One for him as well?"

"Him? He gets nothin'."

Greg knew he had to insult Gosling and get him upset to obtain information, but at midnight the two police officers still had not convinced Gosling to cooperate. A few times Britton thought the man wanted to get something off his chest, but each time it turned out to be a false alarm.

Only when the lab report came in on the blood found in the alley by Madge's garage did Gosling start to come around. Even then he didn't say much.

"That was you bleeding behind Madge's house on the night Sandra disappeared, wasn't it, Vernon? We also know that's your blood on a homework page of hers. What did you do with her?"

"I want a lawyer."

"I said what did you do with her?" Greg asked, standing up, bending over and getting in Gosling's injured face. "What did you do with the girl, you fucking excuse for a human being? What did you do with Sandra?"

Gosling could barely keep his eyes open. "Nothin'. I had nothin' to do with it."

"You had nothing to do with what?"

"I want a fuckin' lawyer."

"I said, with what? You had nothing to do with what? Why do you call her a hussy?"

"Listen, it's my right to have a lawyer here. I need a doctor too ... I'm bleedin' to death."

"We'll get you a..." Britton didn't finish his sentence. The police officer's mind had instantly formed a conclusion. Leaning over the table, Greg's eyes bore right through the face of the human vermin sitting across from him trying to keep his eyes open.

"Jesus Christ, Wally, I've just figured it out. Sandra was referring to this sick son-of-a-bitch, not his son. The girl's diary said 'Brantsen is a major head case. Brantsen means Gosling senior. That was you following her and turning up wherever she went, wasn't it, you lowlife bastard? It was you, wasn't it? You and that maniac son of yours went after her the same way you went after those other girls in the Everton area and all towns north. Your genius son had offices in those towns, didn't he, you sick piece of maggot shit? No wonder Ronnie always had an alibi ... you were sharing the spoils with him. No one ever took your blood and completed a DNA test on you, did they? No, they wouldn't because you were the so-called sane member of the family. Well, we've got your blood now, you disgusting excuse for anything human."

When Greg quickly came around the table, Wally Gaudry stepped in between the two men. Although worry had formed all over Gosling's face, he said, "As usual you've got it all wrong, you fat fuck."

Greg wanted to hammer the individual being protected by Gaudry. "You've been letting that sick-headed son of yours out on his own, and when he started pulling off the same shit as he did in those other towns, you helped him out again and decided to join in the fun. Where is he? He has her, and I want to know where she is! I said where is he? Christ, Wally, let me at this sick prick," Greg yelled, striving to get his hands on the man being protected by his partner.

It took all of Wally's strength to keep his boss away from Vernon Gosling until the lieutenant came to his senses and said, "Okay, I'm all right. I'm going to call you a lawyer now you pathetic wacko. Wally, charge this bastard as an accomplice in the kidnapping of Sandra Potts. If we don't find her, we'll make it murder-one. Now, let's you and I go get our hands on Ronnie Gosling."

"Best of luck, you assholes," Gosling yelled while being taken away. "You won't find him – he's long gone."

As Vernon Gosling was being led to a cell, pounding rhythmic rain on the tin roof of a nearby garage overwhelmed the normal night sounds in the backyard of a mature brown-stuccoed house two blocks south of Greg Britton's residence.

For two months on and off, a crouching dark figure had been patiently watching the dwelling and needed the rain's noise to make his move and enter the basement. The man knew he would not have a problem because his *research* told him the people who lived in the house were all asleep.

Each night after spending time at a particular basement window, the intruder always ever so slowly turned the doorknob of an outside entrance to the room he watched. Most nights the door was locked, but it was always unlocked around one a.m. on Thursdays and Sundays. The trespasser knew why - he had it all figured out. On Wednesday and Saturday nights, seventeen-year-old Robyn Webster used a phoney identification card when she went drinking alcoholic beverages with her friends. When she returned home in the early hours, the young girl was so completely relaxed she always forgot to secure the upper and lower door bolts. After all, nothing had ever happened before, so why would something happen now? She had slept in the room for four years without incident, so tonight like all those other nights when she went out drinking her inebriated mind completely forgot about the bolts and the consequences for not closing them.

The trespasser didn't care about the cold or the rain. He had patiently waited for this kind of weather because tonight beautiful blond-haired Robyn Webster would once again make the ultimate mistake and leave her door unlatched, and he would kill her. No, it wasn't a mistake. She left it open on purpose, just for him.

The girl had to die because she was just another one of those sluts begging him to teach her a lesson. Robyn wanted him to educate her so much, he had to comply. The girl had ignored the warnings of her parents and friends', so tonight, she would pay the ultimate price - Robyn would get what she desired. He would enter her but also choke her as she slept. As she fought, and he hoped she would fight fiercely, he would feel that certain rush – oh, God, an emotional rush so strong his whole body would throb and erupt with voluptuous passion. A personal sensation the Supreme Being only shared with him.

He wouldn't make it quick when he strangled her. If he did that, the whore would die too soon and his rapture would be short lived. No, he'd loosen up, then tighten, then loosen, then tighten, and finally when he *exploded*, he would squeeze her throat so hard, her last breath would be part of sharing God's magnificent offering.

Before creeping to her window, the darkly dressed man wearing a woollen hood waited patiently out of sight for the girl to return home. He took pride in knowing her Thursday and Sunday routines. After necking and petting with her boyfriend, Robyn would wave goodbye before staggering up the path at the back of her house. Once inside, she would turn on the light, close the door, throw her purse and keys on her dresser, her jacket on a chair, kick off her shoes and undress before leaving her room to use the basement bathroom.

Robyn staggered a lot more tonight, the intruder thought, slyly grinning while crouching at the girl's window. She also yawned twice before going to the bathroom. "Aw, my little girl's tired," he whispered. "My little girl is so very, very tired. How fucking convenient for the whore. She had better struggle or I'll be thoroughly pissed off."

The hooded man knew the routine perfectly. This night would be like all the other nights with the other girls, and so far, Robyn had played her part flawlessly. Well, nearly flawlessly. Tonight, for some reason, Robyn had visited the bathroom before taking off her clothes. Still, that alteration to the *script* wasn't important.

After re-entering her room, Robyn sat on her bed and yanked her sweater over her head before throwing it on top of her jacket. The girl's boyfriend had unbuttoned her blouse and removed her brassiere earlier in the car, so the brassier remained crammed in her purse, which Robyn covered when she threw her blouse over it. Next, after gingerly standing, the young girl pushed her pants and panties to her ankles and then sat down again to allow her feet to push the garments onto the floor. After that, she simply leaned back and fell asleep on the right side of her bed.

This sudden change irritated the stalker. He didn't know if he liked the unexpected deviation from the *scene*. Robyn normally crawled into bed and clapped to turn off the light before falling asleep. Not tonight though. For some reason, the naked girl simply fell asleep half on and half off her bed. Her upper body rested on the bed, but her feet touched the floor.

As the nerves in the hooded man's groin tingled furiously, his lips curled a cunning smirk. This scenario reminded him of another time with another girl. A girl he had to kill because she wanted him to kill her. Oh sure, she pleaded for her life, but they all did. All the whores he had *rescued* pleaded for their lives, knowing all along that they wanted to die. It was a game to them. They didn't want to live their filthy way of life; they wanted out with dignity, and he was their liberator, chosen to help them.

He wanted to be in that particular room right now, in bed with the slut who had left the door unlocked waiting for him, but he would stay calm. He knew exactly how long to wait. He would wait half an hour.

As soon as he slowly opened the door and entered, the trespasser quickly turned off Robyn's light and silently closed and locked the door behind him. The room smelled of pizza and stale perfume, and he stood frozen for a moment listening for anything out of the ordinary. Other than normal creaks, the hum of the furnace and the hammering rain, the only sounds in the room were Robyn's gentle steady breathing, and the ticking of a clock.

When he was certain he was safe, the intruder softly closed and locked the inside door the girl had left ajar after visiting the bathroom. Moving next to the girl, he thought her position wasn't that bad after all. She hadn't made her bed earlier; all she had done in the morning was to throw the bedcovers aside. This would make it easier. He would cover her after lifting her legs onto the bed and then she would be snug. If she moved or made throaty sounds, he would know how deeply she slept. First, he would just look at her. Her beautiful hair, sculptured face and neck, full firm breasts and hard nipples, tight stomach, and the way her soft blond haired labia majora skin formed so evenly and so exquisitely around the entrance to her vaginal opening.

Just touching the girl's velvet thighs and lower legs while getting ready to lift them onto the bed aroused the intruder so much he had to stop. He knew if he continued, he would erupt, and that was not part of his *obligation*. He had been ordered to perform perfectly, and he would. It wouldn't be difficult; the girl hadn't moved or made a sound when he touched her. That aroused him immensely.

Five minutes went by before he placed his hood and gloves in his right pants pocket and picked up the girl's panties. They felt smooth when he rubbed them against his face just like the other pairs he had *collected* in the past.

After pocketing his victim's panties, he managed to lift her cold legs onto her bed. She didn't stir, so subsequent to covering her, he gently nudged the girl onto her left side facing the other way. The man knew Robyn wouldn't wake up or make a sound now because the covers would warm her and she would sleep even deeper.

He was right. Slowly moving around to the other side of the bed, he undid his belt and fly buttons before taking off his pants and under shorts. The girl started snoring lightly at first, then more heavily as he slowly joined her beneath the covers.

Highly erect, the trespasser laid on his right side and slipped his right arm under her neck and head bringing her face to his. Next, he used his left hand to cup Robyn's smooth buttocks to slide her against him, touching him, rubbing him. The sleeping girl cooperated perfectly.

Faint soap, shampoo, perfume and peppermint scents gnawed at his senses. Slowly, he gently moved her hair from her face and kissed her eyes, her nose, her forehead and her lips; her full soft easy-plying lips which he played with by placing the tip of his left hand's forefinger in them and moving it from one corner of her mouth to the other.

The voices hadn't told him it would be like this. The beautiful young naked girl in his arms was totally unlike the others. This girl was cooperating like the rest, but she appeared to love him more than they did. She wanted him just as much as he wanted her. Well she would get him all right; every inch of him. He would please her slowly, ever so slowly before he killed her.

Robyn stopped snoring when their bodies touched, but her regular breathing told him all was fine. All would be fine anyway even if she woke up. That's how much she loves me, he thought. That's how much she wants me to teach her. Only he could give her so much more than those pimply-faced teenage jocks that blew their loads in ten seconds before rolling over on their sides and going to sleep.

While the rain played such a sweet symphony, the ecstatic intruder explored the breasts, buttocks and stomach of the devotee lying next to him. She even snuggled her head into his shirted chest and released a quiet rapturous sigh of subconscious delight indicating she enjoyed him firmly and rhythmically caressing the outside of her moistening vagina.

The girl was not about to wake up from such pleasure and as her breathing increased she slowly opened her legs and began moving her body in time tightly against him, almost to point of mounting him.

Two things were not supposed to happen during this euphoric moment of passion. The intruder's mind railed from not being able to control the flow of desire from his monumental erection, and the ring from Robyn's telephone sounded like London's Big Ben.

The first ring didn't wake the heavily sleeping girl, but it did save her life because the trespasser shot out of bed quickly. Hastily pulling on his shorts and pants, he murmured, "I should have slit your throat, you bitch." The second and third rings didn't wake her either, as the man rapidly slipped into his dirty unlaced sneakers, pulled his hood over his face, and put on his gloves while scurrying to the door. It was after the forth ring just as the intruder reached the door when Robyn clapped her light on and released an uncontrollable high-pitched scream that woke up every person on the block.

Greg received the message about Robyn on his way home after interrogating Gosling. Wally had also heard the announcement in his squad car and called Greg's cellular.

"How long ago, Wally?"

"No more than three minutes. Want me to come over?"

"No, there'll be enough cars - I'm nearly there."

Normally Greg Britton didn't drive more than half-a-block south down his alley before parking his car, but tonight he turned east then south for five blocks. Now, only three blocks from the Webster girl's house, he could see flashing lights and substantial police activity taking place. Should he stop? No, he would carry on toward home and check out his immediate neighbourhood. A full report would be on his desk tomorrow anyway. Slowly passing the back of Robyn's house, he waved at officers he knew.

A block-and-a-half from his own house, Greg's headlights lit up the face of a person he didn't expect to see on this soggy night … Wayne Laidlaw.

"Wayne, what are you doing up at this hour?" he asked, exhibiting a curious look after stopping next to his drenched next door neighbour. "Where's your jacket?"

Wayne appeared out of breath from running. "I … I never had time to put it on. I'm attempting to get a police car," he replied, pointing up the alley. "What the hell are they all doing up there? What's happening?"

"Why do you need a police car?" Greg asked, not answering his friend's question.

Laidlaw's eyes remained peeled to the commotion outside Robyn's house, half a block north. "I telephoned the police about ten minutes ago. I thought I heard someone running in our alley and when I got to the backdoor I'm sure I saw a light go on and off in Gosling's house. Jim Potts said someone ran past his place and he asked me to get the police. What the hell's going on behind you, Greg?"

"Another girl has been assaulted," Britton replied, paying particular attention to Wayne Laidlaw's eyes. Not noticing any unusual eye or head movements, he added, "There is a police officer on duty in the front, why didn't you check with her?"

"Like hell there is. She's probably up the road with that mob. I saw flashing lights long before the sirens started?"

"It was a silent approach. You mean no one's watching the Gosling house?"

After nodding, Wayne heard, "Goddamnit, where is she? Well, there's no sense in you catching pneumonia. Get in and I'll take you home."

By the time Greg pulled in his garage and Laidlaw went home, the police officer that was supposed to be watching the Gosling house was on her way back in double quick time. She knew she had made an error leaving her post, and she knew she didn't have an excuse.

Greg Britton allowed everyone working for him leeway to commit two errors. Those on the receiving end of the blast following their third error, usually applied for another local posting or a transfer from the precinct.

"What were you doing up there?" he asked the young female officer. "Your primary responsibility is this house."

"I was the closest when the call came in, sir. I thought I might just catch the guy."

"Did you drive up the alley, or on the street?"

"The street, sir."

"Damn! I'm sure the son-of-a-bitch uses the back lanes," Greg said, finally offering a shrug and a frustrated grimace. "Anyway, there were enough cars in this area to answer the call. Use your head in the future … understand me?"

"Yes, sir."

"Uh, did you go inside the house about fifteen or twenty minutes ago and turn on a light?"

"No, sir. I don't particularly want to go in there, either."

"Okay, Officer Ginetti. Make certain you check the back yard and the alley every fifteen minutes. Oh, er, where's the key?"

"Here in my pocket, sir."

"Let me have it, please."

As the police lieutenant entered the house's front entrance, Wayne Laidlaw appeared behind him carrying a flashlight. "I'm no idiot, Greg. I saw the look you gave me in the alley. And yes, I'm certain I saw the kitchen light go on and off. Do you think I make a habit of jogging at this time of the night … in the rain, and without a jacket? Hell, I don't even jog."

Greg smiled and smacked his friend's back just as Wayne joined him on the same step. "Well, since you're here. Let's take a look around."

Both men searched the house for thirty minutes before Britton concluded, "If young Gosling was in here, he didn't stay very long."

MANIAC

Chapter 9

"So what are you saying?" Captain Sam Csontos asked, sitting with Greg and Wally at Greg's desk in the busy squad room the morning following Robyn Webster's ordeal. All three police officers had arrived early because the chief wanted answers. "Greg, are you telling me that lunatic Ronnie Gosling is on the loose?"

Britton glanced at his partner for a moment before locking his eyes to Csontos' eyes. "I'm saying Vernon Gosling isn't talking, and Ronnie Gosling is missing. Listen, Sam, I believe both Goslings could be connected to the rapes and Sandra's kidnapping. Something's happened to the father's brain and I've asked our psychiatrist to check him out. Last night I…"

Greg stopped speaking and a look of utter disbelief took over his face when he saw Wayne Laidlaw, Madge Grant, Larry Sumislouski, and Jim Potts walk in. Madge had obviously elected herself spokesperson because she waved the hardest giving him signals to speak with them. Within seconds, the four stood at his desk.

"It wasn't Ronnie Gosling that ran down our alley last night," Madge stated, breathing heavily and trying to stare down Csontos. "Ronnie Gosling walks and runs with a limp, and although I didn't see anything I heard that rapist bastard running. It wasn't Ronnie. The person was very athletic. I could do with a beer."

"How do you know how Ronnie runs?" Csontos asked.

"Because when he came back to our area he was out in the neighbourhood all the time. He wasn't that bad after getting out of hospital. He's become a goddamned recluse since then."

"I heard the same heavy footsteps," Larry said, stepping out from behind Wayne. "I was working underneath the Ford, and by the time I rushed to open the doors, he was gone. I looked down the alley and listened, and for some reason I had the feeling he turned right. I followed and when I made it to the street ... nothing."

"What tipped you off he was running down the alley in the first place?" Csontos asked Madge.

"The goddamned barking dogs and the sirens," Madge replied, not caring the slightest about her language. "The second I heard those dogs barking I heard the bastard's footsteps on the loose stones and gravel. By the time I opened my back door, Larry was heading to the corner, yelling, 'Did you see him, Madge? Some son of a bitch just ran by here - did you see him?'"

"Jim joined me at the street and we ran a couple of blocks west," Larry said, "But the guy just disappeared. The bastard lives in this area, let there be no doubt about it. Either that or he parks his car close by."

"It was me who asked Wayne to call the police," Jim Potts said before asking, "Greg, if this guy is out rapin' again, what's ... what's he done with our Sandra?"

Greg appreciated the four coming in, but he didn't know how to answer Jim Potts. Normally such a question would have answered itself, but Sandra's body hadn't turned up, nor had a box full of panties.

"I believe Sandy is still alive, Jim. This person likes the challenge of making his *rounds*. As a matter of fact, he lives to defy the authorities." Exhibiting a frustrated look, the lieutenant added, "So once again no one saw him?"

All seven glanced at one other indicating each was more than annoyed. Finally, after a few more questions, Wally offered them coffee and Greg created a little levity by appointing Madge an honourable detective. The flattered look Madge exhibited got everyone howling, including Madge after she said, "Goddamnit, I finally made the grade, eh, Britton? I'm an actual defective … er, detective?"

"Madge my dear, we needed you all along."

"I know you did, and you had better get a move on before I catch the son-of-a-bitch. He's the same height as that Philip Bayer boy."

An hour later, Greg and Wally sat with Robyn Webster and her parents around the Webster's kitchen table. Robyn had just returned from being physically examined and was told there were no signs of sexual assault. The Websters' knew the intruder had been with their daughter due to the considerable amount of semen on the sheets, and they welcomed the news that nothing else had happened.

It was obvious to both officers that Mr. and Mrs. Webster had scolded Robyn. Besides being embarrassed, the girl's body language indicated she got the message loud and clear.

"Is there anything else you can tell us about him?" Greg asked the nervous girl. "Other than being tall and looking physically fit, did he do or say anything you can remember?"

Robyn slightly shook her head. "So, sir. Like I said, he had a dark hood over his head and he was going out the door when I saw him. When the light came on, my eyes couldn't focus fast enough."

"So he didn't speak?" Britton asked.

"No, but I had …"

"But what?" Gaudry asked, taking notes, and now very inquisitive. "But what?"

The girl couldn't quite get her thoughts together. When she did though, she said, "He must have placed his head on my other pillow because I've smelled that aftershave before. I … I don't think my dad, brother or boyfriend use it, but I'm certain I've … I've smelled it before."

"Was it like the Old Spice I wear?" Mr. Webster asked.

"No, not like yours, Dad. It had more of … It was sort of like a mixture of… Well, it had a sporty smell to it."

"Try and think," Greg said softly. "Think of the boys you know who use aftershave. Do they live around here?"

Robyn's face indicated she was searching every phase of her life where she would encounter such a fragrance. After about fifteen seconds, she said, "I think my grade eight schoolteacher wore it."

"Wore it? How do you know he stopped wearing it?" Gaudry asked, not looking up from his notebook.

"That was four years ago," Robyn replied, still searching her mind. "When we lived in Vanton."

Greg's eyes met his partner's, before he asked, "Vanton? Robyn, how long have you lived here?"

"Going on four years," Maryann Webster said, getting up and plugging in the kettle. "When Andy got laid off, we came here so he could apply for a job at Boeing or Microsoft."

"And you got one?" Greg asked.

Robyn's dad nodded. "Right away at Microsoft. We had no intention of going back there anyway."

"Why?"

While Mrs. Webster set up four cups and saucers, and poured a glass of milk for her daughter, an exasperating grimace came to her husbands face when he said, "I know this might sound bizarre, but there were too many rapes and murders taking place in that area of the State. We got the hell out."

Just as Wally asked Robyn which school she attended in Vanton, and the name of her grade eight teacher, Mrs.

Webster poured four cups of tea and Greg's answered his cellular.

"Britton. Yeah, Mel. You have got to be joking? Oh for Christ's sake. Are you certain? What the...?"

Greg crumpled his face and motioned to Wally. "Er, we've got to go."

"Aw, surely you can take the time to drink your tea?" Mrs. Webster asked, expressing some sympathy that the two were always on the go. The detectives did drink their teas and ten minutes later while walking to their car, Greg said, "The intruder wasn't Ronnie Gosling."

Wally couldn't believe the news. "What?"

"We've been drawing a blank since we started this thing.

The DNA on Robyn's bed sheets didn't match up with Philip Bayer, Vernon Gosling, or his son, Ronnie. But the blood on that page of Sandra's homework was indeed Vernon Gosling's. His blood was also found on the carpet in Madge's bedroom closet, and Allan Dabbit found Vernon Gosling's fingerprints on the basement and bathroom windows of Jim Potts' house."

"What the hell have we got here?" Wally asked.

After the two entered their car, Greg Britton's voice almost became a whisper as they sat there without starting the vehicle. "I don't know, but I'll tell you what we do have. We've got the rapist's DNA but it's not showing up in any existing DNA banks. Any panties he took were clean. I have a feeling the Goslings are his accomplices. Either that or they have Sandra. She almost made it home that night. Someone grabbed her just as she entered the alley. She was most likely grabbed from behind at her gate, and she dropped her homework. The wind must have carried one or two pages away. One sheet blew next to Vernon Gosling as he stood cutting himself behind the fence next to Madge's garage."

"Or it might have already been on the ground when he stopped there," Wally said.

"No, I believe one or both of the Goslings were waiting for Sandra to come home so they could get at her window again. Now, if that's the case, and the Goslings are not involved in her disappearance, then they saw the kidnapper."

Gaudry winced and nodded before stating, "Three people? Jesus, Greg. Madge Grant says she's seen two separate people at Sandra's window. She said one wears a hood and one doesn't; she's never mentioned three. But that could have been one of the Goslings and the kidnapper." Gaudry paused for a moment in deep thought. "You're right, Greg ... if Sandra's disappearance isn't related to the rapist's moves, then she could have been kidnapped by the Goslings."

"Old man Gosling knows a hell of a lot more than he's telling us," Greg said, motioning Wally to start the car. Checking his watch he added, "I think we really have to work on that bastard. Where the hell has this day gone? I'll leave my car downtown - just drop me off at the house."

"Wanna come over for supper tonight? Wally asked. My bride to be is really practicing her cooking."

Britton grinned. "Listen, you've ... er, been buying me too many lunches lately. It wouldn't be fair me eating you out of house and home as well, would it?"

This time the grin flew to Wally's lips. "Yeah, you're right ... I'll take you home. Two steaks always taste better than one."

"Steak? Well, in that case I'll make an exception and..."

"Forget it, you're going home."

"Yeah, that will probably be best. I can't have you serving me steak tonight and buying me steak tomorrow, can I?"

"Who says I'm buying you a steak tomorrow?" Wally asked, knowing he hadn't lost any bets. You just might end up buying me a steak."

"Buying you a steak? When was the last time I bought you a steak?"

"Never," Wally answered, now fully in the mood to take Greg on at his own game. "When it comes to buying lunches ... particularly steaks, that wallet of yours always stays in your back pocket."

"Oh, really? I suppose I didn't buy you a steak ten months ago at the Farmer's Arms Steak House, eh?"

"That's right, Greg. You never did, because I've never been in the joint."

"Wally, you and I went there late last year with Sam and his wife. If I can recall, you even had two desserts. Jeez, for a young man, your memory is horrible. I'm not perfect, but let's be fair here, Partner, will you buy me a steak if I'm wrong? Put your money where your mouth is."

"Sure I will. I have never been in the joint. I really mean it Greg … I have never been in the Farmer's Arms in my life. As President George Herbert Walker Bush once said, 'Read my lips.'"

"Okay then, I'm wrong. Hey, let's try out that new expensive steak house tomorrow. What say?"

"Sounds good to me, Greg old buddy. It's about time we checked it out. This is most kind of you."

"Wonderful, I knew you'd agree."

Licking his lips and cocking his head with pure delight, Wally slapped his hands together. He was still rubbing them when his eyes examined and questioned Greg's expression of self-confidence. Without smiling, both officers stared at each other for a good fifteen seconds until a look of pure frustration captured Wally face. "Jesus Christ, Greg, you got me again?"

"Yeah, but it's getting tougher."

"Er, how about us checking out the Farmer's Arms? It will be a little cheaper?"

Without displaying any emotion, Britton said, "Yeah that sounds good. Now, get hold of Mel and Allan and find out what's happened to those soil samples I requested. Okay, let's go."

Not much was said as Wally drove the lieutenant home. Once again, both men pondered the possibilities concerning Sandra's disappearance, particularly Greg; he knew Vernon Gosling had trailed her many times and was one of the people who had been at her windows. Since Gosling was behind the fence by Madge's garage, instead of being out in the alley, either he saw someone kidnap Sandra, or if he and Ronnie were together, they both saw the kidnapper, or he allowed Ronnie to take the girl. Now the question was, if Ronnie and Vernon didn't taker her, who did. Also, does Vernon know the kidnapper?

Something else bothered Greg while on the way home. He wasn't certain if it originated in the files he read, or someone had said something relating to the case. Whatever it was, it wasn't coming to the surface.

"Front or back?" Wally asked as they neared Greg's house. "Squire's entrance or the servants' door?"

Mickey will be at the back, so the back is fine ... thanks. You'll be in early tomorrow, won't you?"

"Yeah."

As Greg walked from the alley to the end of his garage and Wally drove away, a sprinkling of rain driven by an unexpected wind suddenly turned into a monsoon. The wind was so strong, two empty garbage receptacles standing near the garage went soaring, smacking into the back of his house. Greg followed them and after securing one, he just about had the other one when the wind moved it again. Perhaps the second and third gusts of wind saved the police officer's life. When Greg bent to his right to retrieve the container, it moved again, and stretching his body to recover it prevented a knife from cutting his throat. Instead, the sharp instrument sliced through his outer and inner garments slashing open the top of his left shoulder. Britton hadn't even seen his attacker and a fraction of a second later the same blade came down in another striking motion slicing open the lieutenant's left leg just above his knee.

Being in similar situations in the past, the officer knew exactly what to do. Instead of standing upright and dying as the training films warned, Greg instinctively turned while falling forward and withdrew his automatic pistol. The moment he hit the ground he released two shots at his hooded, darkly dressed adversary now getting prepared to step over him to finish the job. One round must have hit home. The high-pitched ear-piercing untamed shriek the maniac emitted woke up the neighbourhood as he ran across the alley and through the Gosling yard. The intensified scream was so bloodcurdling it made every hair on Greg's body stand on end. Greg went to stand up to chase the yelping figure, but he couldn't. In fact, the lieutenant never knew his leg was cut until he stood.

A few moments later, Wayne Laidlaw was by his side. "Are you okay? The wife's calling 911 for an ambulance and I told her to request a police dog. C'mon, let me give you a hand. Put your left hand around my shoulders. What the hell happened?"

"The fact that I decided to leave my garage door open probably saved my life," Greg murmured as Laidlaw helped him up. Wincing due to the extreme pain of both bleeding wounds, he added, "Obviously the bastard missed my veins and arteries."

Rather than having Greg walk up the stairs in the now pouring rain, Wayne took his friend home and placed him in a comfortable recreational chair covered in plastic in his basement suite.

Greg couldn't get over how nice the place looked. "Nice suite you've got down here, Wayne. When did you finish it?"

"A couple of months ago. We use it when relatives or the kids come and visit us."

Ten minutes later a police dog took up the chase, and Greg Britton was hustled away to the local hospital.

"He ran straight through the Gosling yard, and through another yard across the next street before the dog lost him," Wally Gaudry said, sitting across from Greg in their office. "We've got a sample of his blood because he brushed up against the Caryula house across the street. The bastard's smart - he has his escape routes all worked out. Also, he'd spread a good amount of black pepper at the end of the other yard."

Although Greg had been advised to spend a day in hospital to give his twenty-six stitches a chance to to bond, he had declined the offer and gone home. Whether or not it was the right thing to do was quickly determined when he sat down in his kitchen. Within minutes of him arriving home, Larry and Joan Sumislouski brought over a plate of pot roast with all the trimmings and both of them doted on him to the point of embarrassment. They stayed for over an hour asking what else they could do help, and informed him they couldn't stay in the neighbourhood any longer - that the attack on him was the final straw in making their decision to move.

"I don't mind staying," Joan said, "But I have to agree with Larry, that this isn't the place to bring up our children."

After Larry and Joan left, Jim and Helen Potts turned up with Wayne and Glenda Laidlaw and the four brought more food and a bottle of port. Madge just brought herself and stated if Greg gave her a key, she would keep his place dusted and clean.

As it turned out, Greg didn't go to bed until twelve-thirty. Staggering under the influence of the port and ushering Wayne and Glenda to the door, he said, "Goodnight, goodnight, dear friends. I couldn't have better friends."

Madge drank six strong shots of rum and coke that night and left twenty minutes after the Laidlaws. Staggering a bit as she made her way down the alley, she sang the main Salvation Army hymn.

"He's fast, Wally," Greg said, wincing slightly and shifting in his chair. Even wounded, he's fast. If I hadn't drawn and fired, he would have killed me. That was his intent. Additionally, that squeal of his is weird enough to wake the dead. The guy's a sicko in need of a lot of help."

"You are one lucky cop, Greg. Why did you decide to leave your garage door open anyway? When I dropped you off, I thought you would walk through the building after closing the door. Yet, you didn't. You went through your back gate instead."

"My car was downtown, so I figured there was nothing in my garage to steal. The bastard was waiting for me in the garage. He probably changed his mind when I went along the side. Then when he looked through the window and saw me chasing garbage cans, he silently opened the side door and nailed me. Jesus, that was close. He would have killed me had I been driving. What I can't figure out is why he attacked me?"

"Well, he's read the papers. Maybe he feels we know more than we do," Wally said, adding, "You know as well as I do the lab report states he was the one with Robyn Webster."

"Then that solves our problem," Greg said. "He's got Sandra somewhere."

"Or maybe she's dead." Wally offered.

"Nah, he hasn't left a box of panties yet, but I've got the feeling he's close to doing it. Where are Al and Mel?"

"They're trying to trace the route the guy took after cutting through Mr. and Mrs. Caryula's Yard. They're also checking out fingerprints in your garage. They should be here in a few minutes. If we had kept a guard on the Gosling house we might have caught the son of a bitch."

"I tried, but Sam couldn't spare the manpower. Besides, I've had the locks changed. If Ronnie wants in, he'll have to break a window."

"Where do you think you hit him?" Wally asked.

"In his left side I think. I don't believe I did much damage, but he clutched his left side before shrieking and taking off. Jesus, that sick scream still rings in my head."

"Do you think he'll be back?" Wally asked.

"No, but I wish he would make another visit. He learned his first lesson tonight ... one he won't forget. It's about time *he* felt some pain for a change."

"We've put an All Points Bulletin out to all doctors' offices and hospitals in the area. If he goes to get fixed up, we'll have him."

"I'd like to get my hands on the son of a bitch, but he's too fast," Greg said, chewing his dry lower lip. "also, he's a trained surgeon; he won't go to a hospital."

"Hey Greg, maybe we're looking for an athlete, not Dr. Gosling. What do you think?"

"It's possible ... anything's possible. But have you put two and two together yet, Walter my boy?"

"What do you mean? Have I missed something?"

A devious ear-to-ear smile stretched Greg's lips. "Yeah, no one other than Sam, the Goslings, my immediate neighbours and our crew knew I was working on this case."

"So it means the Goslings are..."

Greg didn't give his partner a chance to finish. "It means the Goslings are definitely working with this bastard ... that's what it means. One stipulation I made when I returned was that Sam would keep my name out of the press. I know your name is mentioned, but not mine."

Gaudry nodded, saying, "Christ you're right, the media has never mentioned you."

"I had a small problem with Helen Potts last night," Greg said, holding his right hand against his forehead.

"Why what happened?"

"She's thoroughly pissed off that Philip is out on bail. She said I'm letting Sandy down. I tried like hell to tell her Philip's not involved but she refuses to listen." Sighing, Greg added, "Anyway, all we can do is our best. Er, are you hungry?"

"Me? Say, uh, Greg ... I guess with you being in this position like you are, we won't be goin' out for lunch after all, eh?"

"Why not? He didn't cut my stomach. Get with it. Shit, I'd have to be dead to turn down a nice free juicy steak."

"Just askin'."

Half an hour later, Allan Dabbit and Mel Holmes entered the busy squad room. They explained they had been at the lab and some weird things were happening.

"Other than yours, there were no fingerprints in your garage, Greg," Dabbit said. "You already know the guy's blood type … and we gave the lab a few samples of mud found on the cement floor in front of your garage's window. That's where the weirdo must have been watching you chase those garbage containers."

Greg made mental notes of the information before asking, "Anything else?"

"Yes. We took more soil samples at the mine, and where Gosling stood behind Madge's fence. We've also sampled the mud at the back gate of Sandra's house, and at the back of the Gosling place. The lab didn't know exactly what we were looking for but they did report what they term as "similarities in certain instances." The mud by Sandra's back gate and by the back basement door of the Gosling house holds traces of clay not found in either yard or in the alley. That clay is not at all similar to samples we took at the mine, nor does it match the soil sample taken next to Madge's fence. Now, here's the good part. Sandra's pants, sweater and shoes all held traces of that particular clay. I propose we start digging up Gosling's backyard."

Grins became contagious as four pairs of eyes met each other head on and Greg asked, "What do you think we'll find there?"

Wally said, "Well there are three blond girls missing in a radius of twenty miles. All are, or were … age seventeen."

"Yeah, but that was three years ago," Greg stated before slowly turning his head and giving his three co-workers questioning looks. Jesus, are you three thinking what I'm thinking?"

"We spoke about that on the way back," Mel Holmes said, pointing at Greg. "When you clued us in to the Everton rapes and murders, three girls disappeared in that area over a three year period and after the rapes stopped, no one bothered to put two and two together."

Staring through Wally, Greg took a deep breath and let it out slowly. "Okay, thanks. Now, anything else?"

"Yeah, the lab found traces of a chemical of some sort on the neck of Sandra's sweater and the front of her windbreaker," Mel Holmes said, reading from his notes.

"Any idea what it is?" Wally asked. "Can't we get closer?"

"The lab's trying, but both items were out in the elements too long. It goes along with your theory, Greg … she was probably attacked from behind."

"Yeah, at her back gate," Greg said, doodling a small dark chemical bottle with a label and writing Wayne Laidlaw sells chemicals - then crossing it out.

"Vernon Gosling was denied bail after I was attacked," Greg stated, slowly standing up, stretching cautiously and gradually sitting down again. "Mel, get a warrant to dig up their front and backyards. I want the job methodically done by pick and shovel. Uh, Allan, I want you to take soil samples at the back and front of Wayne Laidlaw's house. Don't make it obvious. I don't want either of the Laidlaw's to know that it's being done. Got it? When that's completed, I want the both of you to track down the mental health records of Vernon Gosling's parents and grandparents. His mental state must be hereditary. Also, try and find out if Vernon and his son Ronnie had or have any close friends."

"Where will you be?" Mel Holmes asked, standing up to head to his desk.

"Wally and I are heading to Everton ASAP. We'll keep in touch. Oh, hold it you guys."

Holmes and Dabbit returned, and Greg said, "If you've got some spare time, make a random check on houses in the square block of each victim. See if there have been any peeping toms. I figure this son of a bitch really cases his prey. Okay, thanks guys. Wally, I'm going down to the lab. Get Victory Travel on the phone, and get us two tickets to Everton by rail - return open. I don't like those light planes. If there are no trains on that route, get bus tickets."

"When are we travelling?"

"Tomorrow morning. Oh, and we won't be eating today, so you'll save some money. Larry Sumislouski and I will be checking the square block around my house. I want you to check the square block east. Hand out your card and ask if anyone heard or seen people at their windows."

Before Greg Britton made his way down to the laboratory, he removed a phone list from under his desk blotter. Running his finger down the names, he stopped, picked up his phone, punched out the number and placed the sheet away.

"Uh, Good day. Is Lieutenant Roy Rockandel still with your department? He is, but now he's a captain? So, it's Captain Rockandel now is it? Yes, may I speak with him, please?"

As Greg waited, a public relations clerk came over and handed him a file he had requested with all the news releases the department had put out to the media on the kidnapping and rape cases. Greg put the file in his briefcase.

"Roy, Greg Britton here. Yes, it has been a long time, old buddy … How's the Everton Police Department?"

Coughing loudly and shivering out of control in her pitch-black hellhole, Sandra hobbled the few feet of the pipe that held her handcuffed right hand. Trying as hard as she could, Sandra couldn't pull the cylindrical object from the walls. Her strength was failing and she knew her bleeding right wrist was now badly infected.

The young girl didn't know blood from her nose and mouth was smeared with the mud on her face and hair, and her black right eye was swollen and partially closed. While attempting once more to pull the pipe out of the wall, Sandra heard a noise and knew her assailant was coming. Trying to lie down quickly, she slipped and fell hurting her handcuffed right arm. Finding the bed, Sandra covered herself with the threadbare blanket, curled up and gently sobbed.

Paying no attention to the girl's coughs and shivers, when his feet touched the floor, her attacker turned on the single little light bulb and spoke in a very high-pitched voice. "You think I'm a head case don't you my darling?"

Thoroughly dishevelled and spastically shivering, Sandra Potts couldn't answer him. The treatment she had been receiving made her too sick to raise her head.

"You could have had light last night, and I could have turned on the heater, but you've been a naughty girl," he said with a high-pitched voice. "You've been trying to pull the pipe out of the walls again haven't you?

Sandra didn't reply.

"I said, haven't you, you pathetic excuse for a whore? You polluted bitch. You sanctimonious prostitute. I know he's fucking you. And you let him, don't you, you filthy bitch?"

When Sandra didn't answer or look at him, the man pulled her lightly clutched blanket away and yelled, "Answer me or I'll slowly cut your fucking head off. Do you think I would care if I gut you? I wouldn't care. I gutted all the others, so why should I care about gutting you? Just who the fuck do you think you are, parading nude around your room? Well you're not so perfect now are you, you slut? By the time I get through with you, you'll scream that you love me. You'll want no one else but me. Isn't that right, you fucking harlot? I said, isn't that right? Answer me, or I'll..."

It was no use, when the naked girl tried to speak she couldn't. Her mouth was dry from coughing and she had a very high temperature. Sandra felt cold and numb yet she was burning up. Even simple things like the motor control of raising her head had gone, and her captor knew it.

Dropping his pants and shorts to the floor, the man pulled the coughing girl's legs down and parted them before climbing on top of her. "Well, you won't have to worry much longer," he said in his eerie voice. "Your fucking days are numbered, you bitch. Did you get that little play on words you detestable harlot? I said your fucking days are numbered. Then again if you're nice to me I might let you live to fuck again. Would you like that? You've been a poor fuck from the start, anyway but I might let you live. Ha, to think I once looked upon you as a Goddess and..."

Instantly the crazed man stopped speaking and raised his face to the ceiling. "What's that? I can't tell her that now! I said I'm not going to tell her now. Oh, all right! I said all right, didn't I? Now she'll know the outcome. Listen bitch, I've been told to tell you I can't let you go. I was thinking about letting you go, but now I can't – he won't let me. Look at me when I'm talking to you, you slut. You pathetic slut! Look at me, I said!"

Coughing and shivering badly, Sandra slowly raised her head and eyes only to quickly close them again when her head dropped. Her strength had gone, she couldn't breathe properly, nor could she feel the man's weight as he entered her. Coming in and out of consciousness, she didn't even hear the high-pitched squeals of joy the man emitted while thrusting her with his extremely erect penis. Nothing mattered to the girl anymore. The first few days after she was taken she retched continuously breathing in the nauseating smell emanating from her body-waste bucket. Even the smell of urine and excrement didn't matter anymore. The unbearable stench had combined with the damp foul smell of wet clay, dried vomit, and mucus covering most of her body. Sandra's teenage understanding of civility had been won over quickly. Now it wasn't necessary to appreciate why her world reeked so badly, it just did, and that was that. In her hallucinatory condition, she accepted it as the norm.

"Say you love me, you stinking fucking bitch. Say it! Say it! Every part of your body loves me. Say it! Tell me you love me bitch or I'll break every…!"

The semi-conscious girl couldn't tell him what he wanted to hear because she didn't know who she was, where she was, or what he was doing. Since Sandra's bone-dry throat couldn't provide him with the compliment he wanted, the full force of her *jailor's* right fist broke her nose again.

That evening, Larry Sumislouski gave Greg a hand knocking on doors of all the houses in their square block, talking to men, women and children and asking them if they had seen or heard someone at their windows. Some of the people knew Greg and they shook hands. Although neither man had any luck, Greg left his card with all the residents, and on their way home both men stopped off at Jim and Helen Potts' house. Little Merriam opened the door.

"Hello, Sweetheart, are your folks home?" Greg asked. Larry just smiled sympathetically at the sad little girl.

"Hi Uncle Greg and Uncle Larry," she said. "They're in the kitchen."

On the way in Greg gave Merriam an understanding look and ran his hand over the girl's hair before she ran upstairs.

Looking totally worn out, Jim and Helen Potts sat at their kitchen table and smiled through tired eyes as Jim got up to pour two coffees.

"Don't bother, Jim. We're coffeed out," Greg said.

"I'm sorry about last night," Helen said, thinking about the way she treated her friend. "It's just that I can't understand why they would let him out? I think he killed our Sandy, Greg."

Greg took hold of both Helen's hands. "Look, Sweetheart, I know what you're going through, but Philip didn't have anything to do with it. We'll find out who did."

Helen still wasn't listening. With her eyes welling up, she said, "Sandy's blood was on his clothes and you're just like the others ... you don't care. If she was some rich person's daughter the case would be solved by now."

Greg didn't know what to say. "Helen, I promise I..."

Helen Potts couldn't stay in the room. She broke down and went upstairs to be with her daughters. After she had left, Jim said, "I'm sorry, Greg ... but life hasn't been..."

Greg motioned to Larry that they should leave. "I understand, Jim. We'll get to the bottom of this I promise you."

At the front door, Jim said, "We phoned a psychic and she's coming over in the morning. Anything's worth a try."

While Larry placed a hand on Jim's right shoulder, Greg said, "A psychic? I'd like to speak with her when she's finished. Hang in there my friend."

Before Larry went home, Greg thanked him for helping out. "I am beat, Larry. We might not have had any luck tonight, but who knows, we could get a call. Are you working tomorrow?"

Larry looked tired as well. "Yeah, I'm back on my regular schedule … this has worn all of us out."

"I know, buddy. Thanks, and get some sleep. Good night."

"Anytime. Good night, Greg."

MANIAC

Chapter 10

Like children, even grown men enjoy the excitement of being near trains. Whether it's the smoke, the thought of travelling on tracks, the whistles, horns, or just the smell and noise in the station, the sensation signalling the brain that train travel is imminent, creates a stirring emotion within. Greg Britton and Wally Gaudry shared that feeling while listening to the departure and arrival announcements.

"Do you have any idea when you will be returning, sir?" a red-capped conductor asked Greg.

Both detectives wore crisp suits and ties while getting their tickets checked. No sooner had the trainman asked the question, he placed a car number sticker on Greg's luggage and pulled out the Amtrak portions of the ticket.

"One or two days, the lieutenant said, passing his bag to a porter and waiting while another trainman cleared Wally through the same procedure.

"Fine, you gentlemen can now continue to the platform."

Because the train was leaving at 0700, Greg had been up since five-thirty and was ready to go when Wally picked him up at six-fifteen. Checking his watch while limping through the platform gates, it read 0650.

"What time did he say we should be arriving in Everton?" Wally asked, yawning and looking at his watch.

"Close to noon. It's a five-hour trip with stops. There's a dining car so you'll be able to buy me breakfast. This morning I feel like having steak and eggs."

"What?" If looks could kill, Wally's eyes shot daggers. "Now look, Greg, I don't mind…"

"On second thought, Wally, let me buy you breakfast. You're the only person I've ever known who never complains after losing a bet. You know you never have complained. You've always been there with your wallet out ready to pay off your bets. That's what I call class, and that's what I like about you, Wally. You're not cheap … your word really is your bond.

Gaudry genuinely appreciated Greg's straight build up, but the grin on Greg's face also indicated to Wally, there was a punch line coming. At the same time, he never knew what to expect when he gambled with his boss. He never knew when Greg was serious and when he wasn't. This time, like the others, he knew he would have to wait until the end of the meal to see who would pay, and most times, he actually looked forward to the outcome.

After boarding the train and sitting at a table in the dining car, Britton said, "Did you check out the artist's sketch of what our kidnapper supposedly looks like?"

Wally moved slightly back to allow a steward to turn over two coffee cups already on the table and pour coffees. "Yeah, but it didn't do a thing for me. Art the hobo was too high to describe any facial features. One thing was interesting though … no vehicle. How did the person get to the quarry? But then again, he could have parked it around the bend leading up to the parking lot. That way he wouldn't be stuck or reveal his tire tracks. How about you?"

Both officers thanked the steward for handing them each a menu. "Well, I was more curious about the guy's baseball cap."

"Oh really?" Wally asked, perusing his menu. "Why?"

"The colour of the cap is bright orange. No one and I mean no one would buy a cap that colour. It's too bright. I don't think it's a baseball cap. I think it's a golf cap from my golf club and I happen to know Dr. Ronald Gosling has one. The good doctor is an honorary member. In fact, he has two of them. Now I want to know where that goddamned clay comes from. Obviously some of it comes from their backyard, or maybe the another tunnel at the mine we never checked out. It's only about two hundred yards long, but one never knows."

Both men ordered omelettes before Wally asked, "How do you know that?"

"Know what?"

"That there's another tunnel?"

"I didn't return my map to Hank Dabchick. The tunnel is on the other side of the quarry. Trees cover the entrance, but it's there. Apparently the old timers were following a surface vein and it just petered out."

"When did you find this out?" Wally asked.

"This morning. I checked the map over while having a coffee and phoned Hank. He confirmed it."

"Jeez, you phoned Dabchick at six?"

"Yeah, but that was okay, he was up already. I also phoned Sam. He's heading there today with Mel while Allan organizes the dig at the Gosling place."

"Christ I feel like I'm not earning my pay," Wally offered, before thanking the steward for serving his omelette.

As the train pulled away ten minutes late, Greg said, "We should have had this thing solved long ago, and we would have if we had paid more attention to our man's movements. Just think about his movements for a moment. Every house our rapist visited has no back fence. In addition, there no back fences at the rear of the houses directly across from the houses he enters. The only exception is Sandra's place, and to our knowledge he didn't go inside her house."

Wally's facial expression indicated he was tracing the rapist's movements. "Yeah, he knows exactly what he's doing. He cases the joints well in advance. All his victims lived in basements. There are no commercial main streets in the area, and he doesn't park his car in any of the lanes where he makes his move.

"Precisely," Greg said, *digging* into his food. "This guy parks in front of a house in the street behind a victim's house and cuts through, crossing the alley. He probably leaves in the same manner. We had this information all along and we discussed it, but we didn't do anything with it? Had we mapped out the fenceless houses and increased our patrols in those areas, I believe we would have him by now. There are very few unfenced houses."

Gaudry ordered another coffee. "You're right, Greg, but it's hindsight."

"Yeah, it's hindsight but look at the alleys. There are only two, and mine is one of them. My lane stretches nine blocks, as does the alley east, between Alder and Dogwood. The other alleys are blocked by dead end streets."

His partner agreed. "Yeah, I see what ya mean. He's done four on one side and two on the other. The centre of all the action leads straight to…"

"The Gosling place," Greg said, feeling the initial tug of the train. "I've got a feeling that son-of-a-bitch isn't the dodo we think him to be."

Greg grimaced a bit then threw a twenty-dollar bill on the table.

Wally couldn't get over the fact that the lieutenant was actually buying. Offering an incredulous look, he said, "That's mighty fine of you. Thanks."

"Not at all, my boy. I'll buy the breakfasts - you buy the lunches and dinners. No, we'll both buy lunches, but you can buy the dinners."

There were only about thirty passengers in the car to which both men had been assigned. This allowed each a window seat across the aisle from each other, and they took off their coats and jackets and put them up top on the shelves.

No sooner had they settled in their seats, Wally tilted his seat back and decided to grab some shuteye. The lack of people meant a lack of noise, and this suited the lieutenant. Undoing his tie and putting on his glasses, Greg began reading the public information file of news releases.

As Greg examined the dossier, minutes turned into hours until finally he took off his glasses, wiped his eyes, and gazed out the window at the beautiful countryside. He'd taken this trip before, and recollection now captured the moment. He'd been with Diane on that trip, and they held hands while sitting side by side in the dome car. Diane couldn't tear her eyes away from the passing scenery.

"It's beautiful, isn't it, Honey?" she had said.

"Not as beautiful as you, Kiddo."

When Diane slowly turned her head towards him to rest her head against his right shoulder, he noticed her eyes welling up.

"Oh, Greg, I'm so sorry I'm sick."

Greg kissed her hair and gently wiped her eyes with his handkerchief. "You're going to get better, Sweetheart. That's all that matters … the test results on Monday will prove it. I've made special arrangements with a friend of mine named God. He says you'll be back to your old self in no time."

Greg's words brought a faint smile to Diane's face. "I love you so much," she said, taking her right hand and slowly caressing the right side of his face. "If … if I have to go, will you promise me you'll look after yourself, and Jeff, and … Mickey?"

Police officers aren't supposed to show emotion, and as tough as he was, Greg couldn't stop the tears rolling down his cheeks. Wrapping his right arm around her shoulders and holding her tight, he said, "Don't worry about me, Babe ... we'll see this through. You'll get better, you'll see."

Just the thought of that trip with Diane started tears flowing again, and after wiping his eyes, the lieutenant cleared his throat and stared out the window for a few minutes before putting his glasses on and picking up the file again. He'd just started reading where he had left off when a black pistol slowly moved around the seat next to the aisle. The small hand holding the plastic toy led to a grinning little blond haired boy about six who said, "Get 'em up where I can see 'em."

Greg put up his hands. "Are you a good guy or a bad guy?"

"I'm a policeman, and my name's Officer Jeremy."

"That's a nice name. With you police on the job, I guess we passengers don't have too much to worry about. Right, Officer Jeremy?"

"Right!"

A second later Greg heard Jeremy's mother yell, "Jeremy, leave the passengers alone. Come on up here."

Both *men* waved at each other as the happy and smiling three-foot-something police officer left the scene.

The rain might have been following the two officers, because when they stepped out of the station at Everton, the Heavens offered a drenching burst that wasn't forecasted to stop. Fortunately, a shiny black Chevrolet police car waited close by and as Greg and Wally approached it, a grinning Captain Roy Rockandel got out, walked around the front and held out his right hand. "Greg, it's been about nine years."

Greg shook Roy's offered hand and after introducing Wally, said, "It's been exactly nine years, Roy. How come you look the same, while I look nine years older?"

The lean, tall, grey-haired and balding leather-skinned cop laughed. "Country cookin' and the air. Now that the bullshit is over with, good to see ya again. How's Diane?"

"I lost her about six months ago. How's Muriel?"

"Oh, I'm so sorry, Greg. Uh, Muriel's fine. How long will you guys be with us?"

"About two days if that's okay with you?" Greg replied, glancing at Wally who nodded.

"We're on expenses, Roy, so if there's a motel or hotel you can recommend, just drop us there and we'll rent a car. Er, have you eaten, Roy? Because if not, Wally here has offered to…"

Wally's smile widened when the captain said, "There's a motel close to where I live, but you two are dining with us tonight. The wife's cooked a roast and if I remember right, Gregory, you're a roast fanatic provided the meat is well done and horseradish is served mixed with a little mustard. Are you certain you don't want to stay with us? The kids have moved away and…"

Only certain friends called the lieutenant Gregory, and Greg was proud he could call Roy a friend. They had started out together as beat cops before Roy married Muriel who was from Everton. Shortly afterwards the married couple decided to live in Everton and both men kept in touch for a few years. Although the phone calls got fewer as the years went by, they always considered themselves very close friends.

"No thanks, Roy, but the roast sounds great."

Rain continued pounding the streets when Wally and Greg left their motel room and caught a cab to Captain Roy Rockandel's house. Earlier on Roy had told them there was no sense them renting a car because he and his automobile were at their disposal for the duration of their visit. They appreciated the offer but declined the use of it that night.

Hot showers awakened Greg and Wally, and after putting on fresh clothes, they looked forward to Muriel's roast beef and perhaps a morsel of information that could help them find Sandra.

"Uh, you'll not be getting used to this, Wally."

Gaudry knew what was coming and his grin reappeared. "Getting used to what?"

"Not having to buy supper two nights in a row. Had I known we were coming here for supper I wouldn't have bought breakfast."

"It's just my lucky day," Wally said, still trying to see through his boss's play-acting. "You won't deny me this one fluky day, will you?"

"Oh, hell no, Wally," the lieutenant said, keeping a straight face and looking out his window. "But I don't want you to think this is the norm. I really mean you will not be getting used to this. The house we want is the second house on the right ... thanks driver.

Wally wanted to burst out laughing, and actually so did Greg, but both men held their ground as if everything were normal.

As usual, Muriel Rockandel prepared a meal fit for a king, and during dinner, Greg complimented her at least ten times. For some reason, their house reminded him of his house when Diane was alive. The telltale odours of newly baked bread and scones were evident along with that secret house touch only women can provide. The years had also been kind to Muriel and throughout the evening, he gave both old friends fond looks of camaraderie, thinking thank God they had not been torn apart by sickness.

Greg Britton felt thoroughly relaxed being with his pals again and for the first time since Diane's death the world appeared to be opening up its arms for him. At times during the evening, he yearned for Diane to be there, but somehow he managed to compensate for that longing ache without allowing his eyes to well up or letting telltale tears roll down his cheeks. Perhaps everyone's right, he thought. Maybe time will help heal some of the mental anguish I wouldn't wish on any of my worst enemies. Then he remembered what Sam Csontos said at Diane's funeral. "Diane might not be visible, Greg, my friend, but her right arm is linking your left arm wherever you go. After a while, you'll feel her arm let go, and your heart will be at ease. Diane will always be there, but she'll have other things to do in Heaven."

Following dinner Wally helped Muriel clear up a few dishes before joining Roy and Greg in the living room.

"So, Greg, you really think the disappearance of Sandra Potts and those rapes have something in common with our cases here and in other Northern Washington towns?"

"I think so, Roy."

"Well, you're right. After we spoke on the phone, I went into our archives and checked out the rapes and murders that occurred here as well as Cooksville and Breckville. The similarities are uncanny, not only in those towns, but as far west as Port Holmes, Goldfind and Oxford. State Police in those towns had the same luck as we did trying to catch the bastard. Then, all of a sudden, everything stopped. We knew he'd moved, but we didn't know who he was or where he went. In this great computer age and as close as all these towns are, not one member or news reporter put two and two together concerning the boxes of panties."

"You mean each town had its own box?"

"You bet … or its own bag. For example in Oxford, he only handed in two pairs of panties because he'd only raped two girls. There were no deaths in Oxford either. Girls disappeared in Everton, Cooksville, and Mount Coux. Now that was the big one, eight rapes and four missing girls in Mount Coux. All girls lived within twelve blocks of each other, but they weren't friends."

"I bet most of them were blond," Greg said, knowing the answer in advance.

"They were all blond, Greg, and the average age was seventeen. He made an exception for a beautiful young girl by the name of Hillary Axworthy. She was sixteen, and she's never turned up. Connie Simpson was eighteen when two teenage boys stumbled onto her body in a farmer's field. The girl had been missing for three months but the coroner said she'd only been dead two days. Her killer had made a hell of a mess of her face. He likes punching girls' faces."

"You mean he actually punches their faces?" Wally asked.

"Yeah, he punches them so hard he knocks out their teeth and breaks their noses and cheekbones. Nice guy, eh? He hit one girl so hard her left eye had popped out."

Wincing like Greg, Wally asked, "How many girls lived in basement suites or rooms?"

"All of them," Roy replied. "We spent a hell of a lot of money trying to catch the bastard, to no avail. He selects houses with no back or front fences, so when we figured it out, we placed national guardsmen near many of those houses but he seemed to know when they were there and when they weren't."

Greg and Wally just sat there with their eyes burning through the captain. They had heard it all before. In fact, the two were so wrapped up with what Roy was telling them, they didn't notice Muriel bringing in dessert.

"Nothing's changed. The bastard does exactly the same now," Gaudry said, automatically picking up a fork and attacking his piece of apple pie. "Uh, sorry, Muriel ... I didn't mean to swear."

"Muriel grinned leaving the room. "That's quite all right, Wally. I'm married to a cop, remember?"

"You've heard of Dr. Ronald Gosling?" Greg asked, before wondering what the sudden exasperated expression on Rockandel's face meant after the name Gosling was mentioned.

"Forget him, Greg. He had nothing to do with any of these rapes or killings."

"Why do you say that?"

"Evidence. There was no evidence. In most cases, he wasn't in town when rapes or murders took place. He was operating, skiing, or playing golf somewhere. Ronald was always the main suspect, but each time he had ironclad alibis. And with good reason ... no blood of his anywhere, and no DNA on any of the clothing articles. The killer is not Dr. Ronald Gosling. We know the DNA of the rapist, but in a few murder cases there were mixed DNA patterns."

"Well as far as I'm concerned the jury is still out on him, Roy. Tell me, did you compare the names of all people in the specific areas of each town to see if there were any patterns or matches?"

"You bet … nothing. Oh, say, yesterday, human bones were found in a farmer's field eight miles north of town. I want the two of you to look at that crime scene tomorrow; would you mind?"

Wally and Greg eagerly glanced at each other before Britton said, "Hell, not at all. This is good of you. We really appreciate your help. Do you think it's another one of his victims?"

"Oh, yes," Rockandel said, almost dispassionately. "We've removed the remains. When we found them, the bones were resting on clothes. Only shreds remained and our crime lab's workin' on them."

"What about this guy, Patrick Michael Pembroke? Why did you arrest him?"

Roy's face lit up. "Jesus, Britton, you've been doing your homework, haven't you? Good for you. Hillary's blood was found in his truck. The guy got off."

"I know, but how come?"

"Every second of this guy's life was accounted for, and he was just about to get married."

"Did he know her?" Wally asked.

"Barely. He lived a block from her. He apprenticed at her old man's plumbing outfit."

Greg stood up to stretch. His injured leg still bothered him, but with each passing day, the pain eased a little more. "Where exactly was her blood found in his vehicle?"

"A small drop was found on the left side of the passenger seat in his pickup. It was a set up and whoever did it knew both of them. The blood also transferred itself to his clothes."

Greg Britton leaned back in his chair and raised his eyes to the ceiling. After taking in a full breath and gritting his teeth, he emptied his lungs, saying "Son of a bitch."

An ear-to-ear smile covered Wally Gaudry's face as Greg Britton handed the cashier twenty dollars to pay their breakfast bill.

Both detectives had enjoyed their evening with Roy and Muriel and had arrived at their motel around midnight. After a good night's sleep, they answered their wake-up calls at 0800, and looked forward to Captain Rockandel picking them up at nine-thirty.

"That was mighty fine of you," Wally said, with tongue in cheek. "I felt like having the steak and eggs this morning but I thought I'd go easy on ya."

"Hey, you could have had two portions of steak and eggs," the lieutenant shot back most convincingly. "I'm looking forward to some caviar and the works tonight."

"You like caviar?" Wally asked, walking to the lobby with his boss.

"Don't know - I've never tried it. It's too expensive, but if you're buying, why not?" Changing the subject, Greg said, "Wally, have you ever heard of a drug called Nontrapysitate?"

"No, what does it do?"

"It's a blood thinning agent and it goes by a whole bunch of other names as well. When I went down to the lab the day before yesterday, Stu Thompson told me it is entirely possible DNA blood samples could change if Nontrapysitate is taken fifteen minutes before a crime is committed. It's only a theory, of course, but Thompson suggests the book is still open."

"Well wouldn't that be something," Wally said, adding, "I give myself a needle fifteen minutes before knocking someone off and authorities can't be sure of my DNA. Jesus, I hope that news doesn't get out."

"I find it a little hard to swallow too, but..." Greg's ringing cellular interrupted his train of thought. "Hang on a sec."

"Britton."

"Good morning, Lieutenant. I trust you slept well on the noble kindness of our civic taxpayers?"

"As a matter of fact I did. How are you, Sam?"

"Never been better. Greg, that short tunnel at the mine means nothing to us. It's just an empty tunnel and the clay you seem concerned about didn't come from there."

"Okay, thanks. Anything else?"

"Oh, yes. Are you sitting down?"

Greg smiled. "I can take it … go ahead."

Vernon Gosling's mother went nuts, and I mean totally wacko at the age of fifty-one. There's a medical term for it but I didn't have time to give you the lecture. Vernon's father died of a heart attack at sixty-two. Here's something else that's interesting. Vernon Gosling was born in Vanton, and he was a twin to a brother named Arne."

"What?" Greg sat down quickly.

"I said he has a twin brother called Arne. All the farms and pieces of land they own in the Northern Washington area were run by Arne."

"Do other police departments have this information?" Greg asked.

"Not to my knowledge."

"You said, '*were* run by Arne.' Where is he now?"

"In the loony-bin, er… Sorry, that term is politically incorrect these days, isn't it? He's in the Judith Liger Centre in Everton where he's been for eight years, getting out on day or weekend passes whenever Vernon wants to take him out."

"Does he have any kids?"

"Arne's a bachelor, but at one time the authorities allowed him to adopt a boy genius with quite a few mental problems. The kid's first name is Kenneth and apparently, he walked a fine line between reality and imagination. Anyway, Arne raised him to the age of sixteen."

Christ, what a family."

"You bet. Anyway, because Ronald Gosling and Arne Gosling couldn't get along, Kenneth was put up for adoption again and became adopted by a wonderful middle-aged couple named Richardson. They lived in Oxford."

"Where do they live now?" Greg asked, raising his eyebrows while looking at Gaudry's inquisitive face. "Do they still live in Oxford?"

"Kenneth's parents are dead. They died a few years back while on a camping trip."

"How'd they die?"

"No one knows; but we do know both were experienced campers. Mr. Richardson always took a rifle along. They were never heard from again. Bears might have got to 'em because the old man's skull was found along with some clothing but that's about all."

"Jesus, Sam, what are you doing to me? What about his wife, uh, Mrs. Richardson?"

"She was never found either."

Where's Kenneth now?"

"No idea, but the Richardson's brought him up as Kenneth Richardson in Oxford."

Britton repeated the name. "Kenneth Richardson, eh? Anything else?"

"Not yet but we'll keep you posted. You do the same with us, okay?"

"Yeah. How's the digging coming along?"

"Just started on it this morning. We'll let you know. Oh, one other thing, we found traces of ether outside Wayne Laidlaw's garage. I don't think it means much because his car's always full of chemical packets or whatever."

Britton found himself biting his lower lip. "Is there a way of finding out if it's the same type of ether?"

"No."

Before Roy Rockandel arrived, Greg briefed Wally on the information Sam had passed along, and the young detective was stunned. "Jesus, two nuts running around?"

"Yeah, Vernon and Arne Gosling. Now I think we should find this Kenneth Richardson. Er, Wally, how many experienced campers get eaten by bears?"

"Not that many, Greg. Also, let me ask you a question."

"Shoot.

"When Wayne Laidlaw goes on his selling trips, how long is he usually gone?"

"It varies … why?"

"Just wondering."

Captain Rockandel couldn't get over the news as Greg passed along the new information while the four travelled to the crime scene Rockandel had described the night before. When they arrived, yellow police tape cordoned off the five-foot deep hole. After the captain parked the car on a dirt road fifty feet away, the three walked under the tape.

"This is deep. How was it discovered?" Wally asked.

"A leg bone must have worked its way to the surface, or animals dug it up. It's not an old grave" the captain replied, crouching. An elderly local farmer says he keeps seeing some fella slowing down and looking in this direction when he drives by this site. We, uh, we've asked him to sit with an artist, but his memory can't handle it. He also doesn't know the type of vehicle the guy drives."

Just hearing the part about the leg bone started a small arthritic-type pain in Greg's injured leg. "How many times has he seen the guy?"

"He says about three or four times."

"Would the farmer recognize a picture?" Wally asked.

"Yeah, he says he might."

Greg chuckled. "Well we don't have one. Roy, from here, where did the rapes take place?"

Roy's eyes appeared glued to the newly dug hole. "On the edge of town not far from here."

"And where was this girl when she vanished?"

"If this is Hillary, she was on her way home from piano lessons. Her teacher is one of the busiest in the business and he was preparing senior students for their Washington Conservatory examinations. Normally the lesson would have taken place in the late afternoon, say around five-thirty, but he couldn't squeeze her in until nine-thirty. She left his house sometime close to around ten-thirty."

"Find any piano books or music sheets?" Wally asked, shaking his head at the resemblance to his cases.

"Yeah, scattered pages of one book were found in Patrick Michael Pembroke's yard."

Greg and Wally joined the captain as they left the scene. Bending down underneath the tape, Greg asked, "And I take it her blood was found on a page or two?"

"You got it. How'd you know?"

"We're looking for the same fella, Roy. But what really bothers me is…"

Greg's cellular rang. "Britton."

"It's been a fucking slaughter house," Sam Csontos said, trying to control his breathing. Greg, we've got up to four bodies in the backyard."

Sadness combined with a narrow-eyed gaze showed on Greg Britton's face as he bowed his head and kicked a stone. For a good few seconds he couldn't comment on the captain's statement. Clearing his throat he said, "My God, I knew we had a maniac on our hands, I just didn't know the extent of…"

"That's putting it mildly. We'll be going at this dig for another four or five hours," Csontos added. "Greg. I'm afraid to tackle the front yard. When we're finished digging, I'm putting a guard inside the house. Also, many of these victims can't be from this area."

"They're not, Sam. They're probably from around here."

Neither Greg nor Sam said goodbye when they punched off their phones. The shock was enough to make any normal minded adult want to shout. After Britton told Wally and Roy, the three just enjoyed sitting listening to the silence of the car with its motor not running.

Chapter 11

"Are you Arne Gosling?" Greg asked the weirdly grinning man sitting in front of him and Wally Gaudry at the Judith Liger Centre in Everton.

After leaving the burial site, Roy Rockandel decided he would go back to his office to find out how many girls had gone missing in the total area. Before leaving, he loaned Greg and Wally a small pocket recorder along with his car so the pair could visit Arne Gosling. Other than the way Arne combed his hair he looked identical to his brother Vernon, right down to his tobacco-stained fingers.

"I am. Yes, I can tell you I am. He said I could tell you."

"Who said you could tell us?" Wally asked, quietly.

"That's none of your business."

"We're police officers, Mr. Gosling, and…"

It took a good hour for Greg and Wally to chip away at Gosling's barricade until something other than his steadfast cunning emerged. Gosling kept his voice low and never changed his demeanour. "So we had some fun. What do you want, fucking medals?"

"You've had a lot of fun. You and your brother Vernon have been a little busy over these past seven years, haven't you, Arne?"

Just the mention of Vernon's name started Gosling's right eye and cheek twitching and his facial expression indicated he didn't quite know what to do with the fingers on his right hand playing a fast jazz number on his right knee.

Greg noticed the connection between Vernon's name and Arne's nervousness and took advantage. "Or should I say you might have been a lot busier than Vernon … I'm right, aren't I, Arne?"

Now Arne's head started jerking in time with his other disorders and Greg could see defiance giving way to partial compliance. "I help the doctor, that's all," Gosling replied, leaning forward and moving his face two inches from the lieutenant's face. "He's a doctor. You're not a doctor. Who are you? You're not one of my friends. I don't know you. Do I … do I know you?"

"Yes you do know us, Arne. We're also your friends. I know he's a doctor, a damn fine doctor, but how do you help him?"

Arne Gosling brought his knees together "My brother says I can't talk to no one about the girls … specially to people like you who want to hurt us."

"We don't want to harm the doctor or you. We just want to help, that's all. Maybe it's not your brother doing all these bad things to young girls. Maybe it's you. Is it you, Arne?"

With his mouth open and his tongue out, Arne cocked his head back, drooled, and began rocking from side to side.

"I said, maybe it's you … is it, Arne?"

"I ain't never really hurt a girl … they're already dead when he lets me play dolls and house with 'em."

"Who kills them, Arne?"

Keeping his head pointed at Wally's face, Arne moved his eyes all over the room. Fifteen seconds later he replied, "The doctor usually does, but sometimes Vernon does it for him."

"And how do you play dolls and house, Arne?" Greg asked, keeping his voice low and feeling the excitement of a cover-up layer melting away.

"I take off their clothes and we play…"

"House? When they're dead, you let them be the mommy and you're the daddy? You…?"

"I screw 'em. That's what a daddy does, doesn't he? And it feels nice."

As difficult as it was, Greg had to continue asking questions in a laid-back manner. "Do you play house with all of them, Arne?"

"No! No, no, no, no! Oh, no, no, no, no, not me, no, no, no! Only the ones he says I can play with."

"Who gives you that permission?"

"The doctor."

"Yes we know. Does, uh, your brother Vernon like to play dolls and house, Arne?"

"No, he only wants to watch. He likes to look. If Vernon doesn't look, he gets mad and hits me. He helps me bury 'em."

"And does, er … the doctor, also help you bury them?"

"No, he always goes away."

"Where does he go?

"Everywhere. He has lots of offices, but not anymore."

"And you always went … go with him, Arne?" Greg asked.

"No, my brother picks me up and we drive to find the doctor. Did I tell you he's a doctor? Have you ever played house? It feels good to…"

An hour after Greg and Wally finished their interrogation, Captain Roy Rockandel arrested Arne Gosling who was then taken to a police psychological internment centre for assessment. Following that, the captain sent messages to police departments at Cooksville, Breckville, Vanton, Oxford,

Goldfind, Newbridge and Mount Coux, requesting full information on all unsolved rape and murder cases in their areas.

That same afternoon Captain Sam Csontos reported no additional bodies had been found in the front yard of the Gosling house. A twenty-four hour watch was put on Vernon Gosling in custody and the Gosling house. An APB was again put out for the apprehension of Dr. Ronald Gosling.

Later that day, Greg sat with Wally in the Everton squad room reviewing Captain Roy Rockandel's files and making notes. The two were so tired they hadn't even bothered taking off their jackets. Finally, when Roy joined them, Greg removed his glasses and sat back. "Roy, how many times in your career have you known you've missed something on a file? You've read it, you know it's a clue, and know it's there but the goddamned thing won't pop up again?"

Roy pulled up a chair. "Story of my life. Also it's so simple you know you might never see it again? Gimmee a hint and maybe I can help."

"I can't. It's like a starry night when I have my eye on a star cluster. A shooting star distracts me for a fraction of a second, and then I can't locate the stars I was just looking at."

Roy also looked tired as nodded his agreement with his friend. "Greg, I've checked on what you asked. Yes, Doctor Ronald Gosling had offices here in Everton, Mount Coux, Goldfind, Oxford and Breckville."

"Any news from your crime lab on those clothes?" Wally asked.

The captain stood, saying, "That's where I'm going now … wanna come along?"

Even at this late hour, five people wearing white laboratory coats read files, looked through microscopes and spoke quietly in the room reeking of chemicals. The moment Roy appeared, chief technician Howie Mellstead walked over and after being introduced to Greg and Wally, the senior lab-type said, "It's Hillary all right. Her mother identified the ring

Hillary couldn't get off her finger. We're also rushing a DNA test."

"How about her clothing?" Wally asked, taking the ring from Mellstead's hand, reviewing it and handing it back.

"Not much left, I'm afraid. No shoes or socks, but we have pieces of her jacket and skirt. The killer must have thrown them in before dumping her. He probably took her panties."

"Any blood on the items?" Greg asked.

Howie shook his head. "No, and I find that ... odd?"

"What's odd?" Wally asked.

"Well, her blood was found in Pembroke's vehicle and on her music books, but not on her clothing. We've found blue woollen fibres though ... and a chemical of some sort."

"It's ether," Greg stated. "We've been through the blue woollen fibre routine as well. This son of a bitch didn't stop, he just kept moving. Just to be on the safe side, would you mind completing a dental records check."

Roy agreed. "Yeah, Howie, get that out of the way so our asses are covered. Uh, you guys want a bite to eat?"

Greg's grin expanded as if he'd been waiting all day for that question. "You bet we do. Is there a nice expensive restaurant around where that we can...?"

Rockandel didn't understand the reason for the huge grin but it became contagious when he saw Wally copy it a second later. "That won't be necessary, Greg. Muriel phoned and has made supper for us."

Two seconds later, Rockandel couldn't fathom why the grin remained on Wally's face, and mock exasperation filled the lieutenant's kisser.

At midnight just as Greg was dozing off, his telephone rang. For the past hour, he had had gone over the day's activities, including trying to figure out what was subconsciously eluding him.

"Britton."

"Hi, Greg, are you still awake?"

"I wasn't until you phoned. What's up?"

The voice emanating from the phone's earpiece sounded vibrant. "Let's get up a little earlier tomorrow, okay?"

"Why? What's the rush?"

"I'm ordering the *Giant Bushwhacker* breakfast. It's got two steaks and six eggs."

After saying, "Screw you, Gaudry," Greg slammed his telephone down.

In the next room, the junior of the two rubbed his hands together and turned off his light. "That got him. Shit, I finally got to him."

"Well, what do ya know?" Greg said, grinning and lying with his hands behind his head. "The kid is finally learning. He's a good sport."

Just two regular breakfasts and an extra coffee were ordered in the motel's restaurant the following morning. Wally had actually given some thought to ordering the big bushwhacker's breakfast but didn't think he'd be able to handle it. Captain Rockandel joined the duo just as they entered the dining room.

"Anything on who has moved out of that area?" Greg asked, after offering the captain the usual morning salutations.

"My crews are still working on it, Greg. It's a transient area full of old rooming houses. Hundreds move in and out monthly. We've tried all methods of tracing, and so far, no Mr. Kenneth Richardson?"

All three detectives frustratingly shook their heads as Roy's cellular rang.

"Good morning, Captain Rockandel here."

Greg and Wally kept on eating but watched the concern growing on Roy's face. "What do you mean? Give me her name. That's easy enough to remember. Anything else? Oh, Really? Is he certain? Okay, thanks."

Roy placed his cellular back into his pocket. "The coroner says he doesn't believe Hillary was murdered right away. She'd suffered a cracked cheekbone, fractured ribs, and a broken arm and nose. He's not certain yet on the cause of death."

Disgusted, Greg said, "So she was another one the bastard held as a plaything until he captured the next one?"

"Looks that way," Rockandel said. "C'mon, we're going pick up her medical and dental records. Some dizzy assistant won't release them without a court order."

Greg stood up to leave. "Ya gotta be joking? Where's Everton's community spirit?"

"Same as everywhere else - in the bank. Next, they'll be charging us for medical and dental records," Roy said before picking up the check and reviewing it. Placing it down with a twenty, he added, "Breakfast is on me."

Greg tried to hide a grin while putting on his coat. The only word he'd heard from Wally was, "Damn."

After rubbing his hands together, Greg smacked Roy on his back and said, "That's mighty nice of you Roy. Wally is going to be buying us our evening meal."

"Can I help you gentlemen?" a young female medical receptionist asked Captain Rockandel, when the officers entered a brightly furnished medical/dental office on the third floor of a building on Everton's main street. Greg noticed the entrance door divided two receptionists in a waiting room. A man and a woman sitting waiting for their appointments were laboriously reading copies of *Medicine Now*.

"Is Dr. Stein in?"

The good-looking black girl smiled. I'm Dr. McFarlane's receptionist - you need the girl over there on the other side."

Roy quickly checked his notes. "No, you'll do," he said lowering his voice. "One of my assistants phoned about picking up copies of Hillary Axworthy's medical records and someone here told them there would be a problem."

"I can't understand why," the young woman offered, reaching for an envelope with the police officer's name on it. "Are you Captain Rockandel?"

"Yes."

Remorse came over the receptionist. Handing over the envelope, she said, "Here you are Captain. Those are all the records we have. Hillary was an extremely healthy and beautiful girl. I still say prayers for her.

"We do the same, thank you," Rockandel replied, ushering Greg and Wally over to the second reception desk. "Is Dr. Stein around, please?"

The second girl wasn't as pleasant. She appeared to be in love with herself and her position. Facing Captain Rockandel but raising her chin and talking with her eyes closed, she said, "He's with patients, but he finishes at five pm. Please telephone for an appointment."

Greg had to intervene. He hated people presenting their holier-than-thou attitudes. Forcefully he said, "We're not concerned about his fees, my dear; we're police officers and we need to speak with him *now*."

Appearing sociable, but still defiant, the receptionist was not about to be pushed around. "Like I told you, he's…"

The doctor just happened to be coming out of one of his examination rooms. "That's fine Miss Martin. "I'm Dr. Stein; can I help you gentlemen?"

Roy presented his badge. "Captain Rockandel. I've been told your office refuses to allow us to look at Hillary Axworthy's dental records unless we present you with a court order. Is that true?"

The balding middle-aged professional wearing light green clothing and a lowered paper mouth and nose mask glared at his receptionist. "Did you tell them that, Miss Martin?"

"Well, I might have … I thought…"

Obviously, Dr. Stein had put up with Miss Martin's attitude previously. "I'll speak with you later. "Er, we don't have Hillary's records. Hillary was an irregular patient of Dr. Robert Baylis, and when he sold me his practice, only permanent patients' records were left with us."

"That makes no sense," Greg stated. "Where's Dr. Baylis now?"

"Practising in New York. It does make some sense in that the purchase price of this practice was based on the number of permanent or should I say regular patents. I believe I have his number; would you like me to have him fax the information to you?"

Roy agreed. "That will be fine ... very kind. I'll be back in my office within the hour."

As the three officers left, they heard Dr. Stein say, "Miss. Martin, please join me in my office."

A black tarpaulin of swirling clouds released a downpour that pounded the region as the detectives drove to the police station.

After asking Roy for Hillary's medical records and glancing over them, Greg Said, "The young lady was right. Hillary had a few colds and tonsillitis, but not much else. Her mother would not allow her tonsils to be removed, and as it turned out, they didn't have to be removed. According to the chart, there were no marks or scars on the girl. She was in perfect health." He passed the four documents to Wally."

"If we catch her murderer, I just want one minute alone with him," Rockandel said, before adding, "No, make it fifteen seconds."

Both men chuckled, but not Wally. "Uh, Greg, did you check these signatures?"

"No, why?"

"They're signed by Dr. Ronald Gosling. She was just a kid when..."

Captain Rockandel pulled the car over just as Greg said, "What?"

Ten minutes later, all three were back in the medical building speaking with Dr. McFarlane. The doctor told them when Dr. Gosling came down with a mental problem his practise was put up for sale.

"So you travel to those small towns, do you?" Greg asked.

"Yes, I have a strict schedule that I follow. If my staff members are not here, the dental receptionists answer my phones. I feel very sorry about Dr. Gosling. I certainly hope he improves. Could you gentlemen wait a moment; I've got some chemicals being delivered by Charter Chemicals and Drugs."

"Charter Chemicals and Drugs?" Greg asked. "Would you mind telling me the name of the salesman?"

"Sure, it's Mohammed Bhamji. He services most of the medical offices in Northern Washington State. Do you know him?"

Instantly, Greg's throat and lips went dry, and trying to lick his lips didn't provide any moisture. "Doctor, how long has this Bhamji fella been providing you with products?" Greg asked.

"For about six years. It used to be a fellow named Wayne Laidlaw, but he apparently decided he wanted to service the more lucrative southern part of the state. Now if you'll excuse me please."

"What's the matter?" Roy asked. He had never seen Greg's face so focused yet ashen.

"If it walks like a duck, it's a duck. It's too much of a coincidence," Wally said. "This guy Laidlaw lives next to Greg and across from the Goslings. We highly suspect someone's been working with the Goslings, we just don't know who."

"There's only one problem," Greg stated. "Laidlaw wouldn't have served this area when the kidnappings and murders were taking place. He wouldn't know anyone in this building."

Wally didn't agree. "C'mon, Greg. Wayne Laidlaw knows this area like the back of his hand; he could come here at any time.

"Have you got a picture of Laidlaw?" Roy asked.

"Yeah, and I want you to show it to that farmer who lives close to where Hillary was found. Has your department got a light plane or helicopter that can take us back?"

"We always have a plane on standby. What about your bags?"

"Send them to us along with the bill, Greg said, taking out his cellular. "I think there's a possibility Gosling is living in Laidlaw's basement suite."

Greg punched out Sam's number, and placed his hand over the mouthpiece. "That's the guy Art the hobo saw wearing that golf cap. Hello, er, Sam, it's Greg ... I need a favour. Go to my golf club and take down the picture of Jim Potts, Larry Sumislouski, Wayne Laidlaw, and me. It's thumbtacked to the wall by the bar. Enlarge it when you scan it, and send it by email to Captain Roy Rockandel at the Everton Police. His email address is in my rotary file. How long will that take you? Super! I'll be in touch ... we're on our way back now. We're going to land at Piper's Field not the main airport. That's only five minutes from where I live. No, don't stake it out. For some reason when we plant a stake out everything goes wrong. Yeah, probably a twist of fate but let's not take any chances. Is there still a guard outside the Gosling house? Good. Do you have a car that can pick us up at Piper's Field? Great ... I'll get back to ya."

With its red light turning, Roy Rockandel's car moved through traffic at speeds touching eighty. Picking up his radio's microphone, Rockandel said, "Priority, One-Fiver."

A female police radio operator answered, "One-Fiver, go."

"I need Bravo-Niner fully fuelled and ready to fly in fifteen minutes."

"Roger One-Fiver, wait."

Roy slowed down a bit as the sky continued to release all it could. Even the windshield wipers couldn't clear the rain fast enough.

"One-Fiver, Bravo-Niner, set."

"One-Fiver, thanks ... out."

"Does that mean we're okay?" Greg asked.

"Yeah, you've got your plane. You'll have a tailwind too, so I figure it will only take you about an hour and a half to get home."

"Great night to fly, eh, Wally?" Britton asked, not waiting for a reply as he took a business card out of his wallet. "Roy here's my cellular number. After the farmer sees that picture, phone me please."

Greg Britton hated light planes, and he hated them even more flying in wind and rain during late afternoons when he couldn't see much.

Red, green and white strobe lights lit up the surrounding area and two engines hummed as Roy Rockandel drove on the tarmac towards the Everton Police Department's twin-engine Cessna. There was little time for shaking hands, but thumbs up signs and rushed mock salutes expressed friendship and professional courtesy as Greg and Wally ran towards the aircraft. They were soaked by the time they entered, and the pilot made certain they wore their seatbelts and headsets properly.

Shortly, headlights lit up the runway as the plane taxied, took off and turned south.

All three flyers indicated the bumps were uncomfortable, but the pilot said the turbulence shouldn't last long, that the low-pressure ceiling only existed around the Everton area. By the time the pilot offered a thermos of hot coffee and an ample selection of assorted sandwiches and donuts, the jolts had stopped and the ride was relatively smooth going.

There was nothing to see during the trip, and Wally fell asleep quite quickly. Britton couldn't sleep; he still didn't trust small planes, so he allowed his mind to cover the day's activities and tried to remember certain points in the files he'd read. All signs led to Wayne Laidlaw, particularly his words at the barbecue. *"The way Sandy is developing, I'd be concerned. You'll need double locks! The way Sandy is developing, I'd be concerned. You'll need double locks! You'll need double locks! You'll need double locks!"*

"Thank you Mr. Laidlaw. You're the first totally cool adult to notice I'm growing up. Thank you Mr. Laidlaw. You're the first totally cool adult to notice I'm growing up. Thank you Mr. Laidlaw. You're the first totally cool adult to notice I'm growing up."

"Sandy, what are you doing? Do up your top!"

Greg remembered it all so well, even Helen's concern and Wayne rushing over, straddling the girl, and trying to pick her up by her waist. *"Growing up? If I was fifteen I'd be camping on your doorstep. Growing up? If I was fifteen I'd be camping on your doorstep. Growing up? If I was fifteen I'd be camping on your doorstep."*

"Help! Stop it, I totally like it! Help! Stop it, I totally like it! Help! Stop it, I totally like it! Help! Stop it, I totally like it!"

Although Wally woke up and the pilot gave Greg an odd look, neither one knew Greg hadn't heard himself yell, "We've got you, you son of a bitch, and I'm going to personally rip out your nuts."

Twenty minutes later, after the small plane's wheels screeched hitting the tarmac Greg and Wally said goodbye to their pilot and sat in the back of a shiny black ghost car on their way to Laidlaw's house. Water on the ground indicated it had rained heavily, but the wind was pushing the clouds east and a few stars were beginning to twinkle. Still both detectives knew the rain would be back.

Ten minutes from home the car went over a very hard bump and the jolt forced Greg to open his eyes wide. The revelation he'd been waiting for had arrived with that jolt. All those hours of reading files but not seeing anything worthwhile had come to the forefront of his mind. Now it had happened, the star cluster he'd mentioned to Roy was in focus again. The main clue his subconscious mind had been working on day after day had erupted with the zing of a hundred marching bands. When his cellular rang, he answered saying, "Hello Roy ... I know what you're going to say."

It was Roy, and he asked, "Greg, how did you figure it out?"

"Remember I asked how many times in your career you've known you've missed something on the file? You've read it and know it's there, but the goddamned thing wouldn't pop up again?"

"Yes."

"Well it arrived and it couldn't have come at a better time. If I said to you that the farmer took a look at the photograph and said, 'That's him … it's Dr. Baylis.' Would I be right?"

By now, Wally had his face two inches from Greg's head. As close as he was though, he couldn't hear Captain Rockandel say, "Right on, Gregory and it's been verified by Drs. Stein and McFarlane.

"Keep this to yourself, Roy, old friend. We'll arriving there shortly and I'll call you."

Greg Britton's fist tightened as he looked at his reflection in the window and allowed his mind to return to the barbecue and echo the killer's words. *"They can't. He wears a blue woollen hood. They can't. He wears a blue woollen hood. They can't. He wears a blue woollen hood."*

"How goddamned stupid I was" Greg muttered, hearing the words, *"Tell me about it. I'm always cleaning mud out of our basement, mud out of our basement, mud out of our basement, mud out of our basement."*

Greg Britton felt closed in again and he lowered his window all the way. He wanted to jump out of the car to ring a neck that should have been rung long ago. Sloppy DNA reporting could have saved a good many of the girls, but no, the laboratories made certain they just reported the facts.

When Greg's cellular rang again, he thought it might be Sam but it was Roy again. "Greg, it's Roy. Five of the victims used Robert Baylis as their dentist. We can't track the others … they've moved."

"Did you check him out in New York?"

"Yeah, not listed."

"I think this bastard has or had many other aliases. Thanks, Pal, I'll be in touch shortly."

While on his cellular, Greg had not noticed the route the driver had been taking. By taking a left instead of a right at the last light, they were on a one-way viaduct that took them miles out of their way. "Driver where the hell are you going?"

"Sorry Lieutenant, I wasn't thinking."

"Right now we're not paying' you to think. Get a goddamned move on and turn this heap around."

Sandra Potts at least had light as she shivered on her bunk. The girl's eyes had been blackened; she had a broken nose, fractured cheekbones and a fractured left arm. Dried matted blood covered her hair and was visible all over her bruised body.

Cowering when she heard a noise from up top, the girl quickly drew her feet in under the blanket. A moment later, the trap door opened and the unlaced sneakers of her hooded captor climbed down the ladder. Something was different this time. The girl saw him carrying a two-foot piece of rubber surgical hose in his left hand.

Before her kidnapper arrived at the ladder's last rung and turned towards her, Sandra grabbed the steel thermos bottle with her right hand, and hid it behind her, next to the wall. The small gap between the bunk and wall allowed the item to remain unseen.

Intentionally menacing the terrified girl, the hooded figure moved closer wrapping the hose around each ungloved hand and stretching it.

"No, no ... no more, please," she begged, sobbing and pushing her body back, to no avail.

Ignoring Sandra's pleas, the hooded figure grabbed the girl's feet and pulled her legs down and open. As he reached to rip off the blanket, the girl pulled her legs back.

"Please, please don't. No more ... please?"

"I'm in no mood for fucking defiance," the hooded man squealed, dropping his pants and shorts to the floor. Before laying on her, he yanked her feet down and parted her legs. This time the man's body partially shielded Sandra from the thermos as he pulled off the blanket and climbed on her. With his hands pressing the rubber hose across her neck, the girl could hardly breathe or move. Knowing she could not reach the thermos or move her right hand, in great pain,

Sandra pounded his face with her left hand and pulled off his hood, recognizing him instantly.

"You … it's you … it's you! Why are…?"

Sandra's half-closed eyes became wild as she scratched her left hand's fingers down her assailant's face and chest.

Releasing the hose from his left hand, the man screamed in agony and instantly slugged her hard across her face, knocking her out for a moment.

Seeing that she was unconscious, Sandra's attacker removed his hands from her and unbuttoned his shirt to check his wounds. What seemed like hours to the girl were really seconds. Sandra slowly opened her eyes and little by little placed her right hand on the thermos. In one swift upward move, the girl slammed the device hard against her assailant's left temple, instantly stunning him. Newfound strength entered the girl's body and she hit him repeatedly, knocking him out, but losing the thermos to the floor.

With the limp man's his dead weight laying on her, the girl used all her energy trying to get her shaking right hand into his shirt pocket to find the handcuffs key. She found it and struggled to shift his weight as she nervously tried to unlock her cuffed hand. The lock wouldn't open and she tried again, but it still wouldn't open. Noticing her captor was moaning while gaining consciousness, Sandra tried repeatedly. Finally, it opened and she pushed him off and made it to the ladder. When she neared the top, she pushed the trap door open.

The maniac didn't take too long to regain consciousness and grab Sandra's feet on the upper rungs and partly pulled her down. He still held the rubber hose in his left hand and somehow Sandra knew he planned to kill her. This was it - there was no second chance and she understood what she had to do. Using every bit of her energy, the girl freed her right foot from his grasp, brought it up and kicked his face so hard, the action forced him to release her. Her respite was only temporary because once again her assailant grabbed her ankles and began yanking her down. Sandra reached for anything she could grab and somehow managed to seize a full tin of paint and swung it down slamming her attacker's face. The object hurt the man and forced him to slide down the ladder. By the time he came after her again, Sandra was up top.

Sandra Potts didn't know it at the time but she loved the feel of the rain hitting her face when she flew through the open doors of Larry Sumislouski's garage and flung herself into the arms of Greg Britton approaching the building. Greg found the nude girl sobbing frantically, unable to talk, breathing heavily and wildly flailing her arms in the direction of the doors.

Quickly removing his topcoat, Greg wrapped it around the hysterical girl and gently passed her to Wally saying, "You're okay now, Sweetheart. You're going to be just fine."

Raging and making deep howling guttural noises, Larry Sumislouski came out of the garage like an uncontrolled bull heading for Sandra with a piece of surgical cord stretched between his hands. The lunatic didn't care who was present, he had one thing on his mind and that was killing Sandra. Wally turned his back to the man to protect the girl, but Greg Britton didn't. Bringing his right hand back at least two feet, the fist's forward motion had the officer's full weight behind it when it ploughed into Sumislouski's face, almost knocking the maniac's head off and sending him flying backwards onto the Ford's hood.

That wasn't enough for the enraged beast. Spittle and blood shot out of his mouth as he screeched, "You fucker, Britton," and employed the same cold-blooded intense shriek he had used a few days earlier. Sumislouski came at the officer with just as much speed and ferocity that a man can muster. Unfortunately it was all for naught, because Greg's left and right fists tore into the man's face again with such vicious intensity, the propelling force shot the wild animal back against the ford knocking him out. A moment later, however, the guttural wailing started again and Sumislouski tried to get up the third time but Greg grabbed him by the hair and after literally dragging him to his feet and giving him a punch to his stomach, the officer hammered the maniac's head hard against the car's hood.

Holding Wally tightly and crying into his shoulder, Sandra hobbled up the path to an overjoyed sobbing mother rushing towards them with outstretched waiting arms.

Stepping away from the car, Greg knew he had seen something a second or so earlier, and as he glanced to his left, Sumislouski's little boys stared at him through sad and searching eyes. They held a green plastic garbage can in their tiny hands and they had seen the whole thing. Offering a sympathetic look, Greg said, "Your dad did a very … bad … Go back to your house boys. Away you go."

When the boys turned and ran, only the sounds of the rain and Sandy and Helen's sobs mixed with the lone flashing red light clicking in the alley. Shortly, the thuds of Dabbit and Holmes' running feet came towards Greg and the police driver who was on his radio obeying Greg's order to "Get a police ambulance with a straight jacket."

Greg stepped back just inside the garage to see a small workbench on its left side, revealing an open trap door attached to its legs. When he tilted the bench upright resting it on four legs, the trap door covered the opening.

"The bastard built a room below his garage. The car meant shit," he mumbled.

Sam Csontos arrived moments later, and the fat captain with a grim face shook Greg's hand. Soon, so did Madge Grant and the two Laidlaws. Obviously, Roy Rockandel had briefed Sam because he didn't ask too many questions other than, "Have you spoken with the son of a bitch's wife?"

Greg shook his head. "No, not yet, but I will. She had no part in this; he had her fooled just like he fooled everyone else."

"Do you have any idea about the whereabouts of Dr. Ronnie Gosling?"

"I didn't until I was on the plane. I think you'll find him in the basement of his house in a hidden room with the door just under the stairs. I forgot it was there when I searched his house. The same contractor built my house and the Gosling house and he constructed a fair-sized preserves room in each basement."

Turning towards Dabbit and Holmes, Britton said, "You may as well pick up Dr. Gosling. Go easy on him; I don't believe he played any part in this."

Five minutes later, clean shaven and neat looking, Dr. Ronald Gosling, wearing jeans, loafer shoes, a plaid shirt, and a brown windbreaker was led out of the house into a waiting police car. The only thing he said to Dabbit and Holmes was, "I'm glad you caught them. Will I get help to get back on my feet?"

Mel Holmes said, "Yes, sir, you will. You'll be well taken care of and you'll receive the help you need."

At eleven-thirty that night as Greg turned his key in his lock and opened the door, his telephone rang. It was his son Jeff.

"Yes, they moved some bodies here, son, but we don't have an exact count. We'll know in a few days, and I'm certain we'll find more bodies up north."

"So even after he moved, he kept going back to Everton to rape and kill, eh, dad?"

"He had to, son. He told his wife he was going to buy parts for his Ford, or to talk to other dentists on new techniques, but he had two girls locked away somewhere. We'll find out. I'm only sorry we couldn't save them. Hillary Axworthy was his second latest victim, and although we were getting closer, we couldn't save her. These bastards were really well organized. Somehow, Vernon Gosling teamed up with his brother Arne, and Arne's adopted son. Can you believe that? Most times Vernon and Arne Gosling where the lookouts while Larry stalked his prey. Only Vernon Gosling and Larry Sumislouski killed, and I believe only Larry Sumislouski, or whatever his real name is caged his victims and continually raped them. Before he became Larry

Sumislouski, he used the names Kenneth Richardson and Robert Baylis."

"But what about Ronnie Gosling? He must have known he was sharing offices with his uncle's adopted son?"

"Sure he did, but so what? He didn't know Vernon, Arne, and Larry were raping and killing girls. A lot of Arne's weirdness must have rubbed off on his adapted son all those years ago. Actually, the kid was crazy anyway. I think we'll find he killed the old couple, uh, the Richardsons. Quite a family, eh?"

"Sumislouski's twin sons, or whatever his name is, will have to be watched as they get older ... you know that don't you, dad?"

"Yeah, I spoke with Sam about them tonight. Uh, I'll pick you up tomorrow at the bus depot."

"Thanks dad. I'm really proud of ya."

"The credit goes to you for tipping me off, Charlie Brown."

"Does this mean you're goin' back to work?"

"Never thought I'd say it, but ... yeah."

"What about trips to the cemetery?"

"I'll work them out. I don't look forward to writing the report on this case."

"I don't blame ya. Well, Goodnight pops, I love ya."

"I love you too, son. Goodnight."

After Britton took off his damp coats, he placed them over a chair back, opened the fridge and took out a beer. Sitting down again after taking a swig, he picked up his phone and punched out some numbers. "Hi, Jim ... it's Greg. How's Sandra?"

The grin on Greg's face indicated Jim was on the mend.

"Helen's with her in the hospital. She's going to be all right. Greg, I..."

"You've thanked me enough, Jim. Say, I was going to ask you what did the psychic say?"

"She drew a picture of a work bench on its side."

"Look similar?"

"Exactly the same. Are you comin' over tomorrow?"

"Yeah, and I'm goin' to the hospital with you. Good night, old friend."

Greg thought he heard Jim's voice turn a bit nasal, and he knew the man was crying tears of happiness when he said "Goodnight, Greg. Thanks again and God bless you."

It was quiet in the alley except for the clicks of flashing red lights attached to vehicles bringing police and their photographers to investigate the hidden hellhole below the garage. The silence didn't last long, though, because the sound of a scratchy phonograph needle preceded the turned up voice of Della Reese singing, *Don't You Know.*

Five minutes later after putting the record away, Greg cracked open another beer before saying, "Whatsamatter with you, Mickey ... are ya hungry? C'mon, I'll feed ya."

The following morning, Captain Sam Csontos sat completing paperwork in his office when his phone rang. The captain was in a good mood. Earlier he had told Greg, "Nothing, absolutely nothing, can ruin my day today." Picking up the receiver, he said, "Good morning, Captain Csontos here."

An enchanting female voice said, "Captain Sam? Oh, what a masculine voice. A friend of yours said I should call you, and..."

On his way past Greg's desk, Csontos *sang*, "That was mighty nice of you guys. She just called me and I'm taking her to lunch at a real fancy restaurant. If her body is like her voice, I've got it made."

"Er, who called you? Wally asked, questioningly.

Humming softly to himself, Csontos combed his thinning hair and straightened his tie. Glancing at his tongue in a nearby mirror and spraying four shots of peppermint into his mouth, he said, "I believe she said her name was Bonita Cigarillo or something like that." Before leaving the squad room he chirped, "Thanks guys, I owe ya one."

Nothing was said until Greg's impish grinning eyes met Wally's wide questioning eyes.

"You called her and gave his name and number? Jeez, Greg, that's the lowest dirtiest trick you could ever…"

For the first time in six months, Greg Britton's laugh could be heard all over the squad room. So could Gaudry's, when Greg said, "Never mind what Bonita-Thelma's gonna do to him, I wanna see the Captain's crotch when President Clinton gets through with it."

OTHER NOVELS BY CORDELL CROSS

REVISED ISBN - ISBN 978-0-9696248-5-1
STAND BY YOUR BEDS! is the hilarious story of seven 14 year old army cadets
sent to a summer military camp for six weeks training. The camp holds 2000 boys,
so to survive, the seven call themselves the musketeers. Regular Force instructors
returning from WW2 and the Korean War are sent to the same camp thinking
they would be training officer cadets. When they discover that the boys are only
fourteen, it doesn't matter - they are there to be trained. In a way, though, the
boys also teach their instructors a few things about life. Extremely funny. Get
ready to roll on the floor, laughing.

REVISED ISBN - 978-0-9696248-7-5
NEXT STOP, VERNON! It is their second year at the Vernon Military Camp,
and the musketeers are much more prepared for military life. Or are they?
Brilliantly comical, so get ready to hold your stomach again.

REVISED ISBN - 978-0-9696248-6-8
FORM THREE RANKS ON THE ROAD! It is three years later, and the
musketeers continue their capers. This time they are in charge, or so they think. A
refreshingly funny book.

REVISED ISBN - 978-0-9696248-8-2
THE HIMMLER STRATAGEM
A must read if you enjoy fast moving suspense, intrigue, and mystery in a world of
intense hatred and sleaze.

REVISED ISBN - 978-0-9869503-0-8
MANIAC
When a sixteen-year-old girl disappears in the neighbourhood of Greg Britton, a
Seattle police lieutenant on compassionate leave, the police officer holds nothing
back and decides to find her, dead or alive.

MAP FACTS
ISBN 0-9696248-3-2
The ultimate map and compass guide, is required reading for all those involved
with topographical maps and magnetic compasses.

Watch for RUBBER GEARS NEXT YEAR!
It is the fourth and last novel in the Vernon Army Cadet Camp series.

COMING SOON FROM CORDELL CROSS
WHERE THE WIND HIDES
RUBBER GEARS NEXT YEAR
RAIN ON YOUR TONGUE
THE STOPOVER